THE SWAN SANG ONCE

Also by
MARJORIE CARLETON

CRY WOLF

THE

Swan Sang Once

BY

MARJORIE CARLETON

WILDSIDE PRESS

A condensed version of this book appeared in the
American Magazine under the title of
"The Dreadful Strangers."

To

AYA AND SKID

THE SWAN SANG ONCE

1

THE MORNING was quiet and except for a hurrying figure in the far distance the two of them had the street to themselves. They moved with surprising agility, considering the conditions, for the street was under repair; and the heavy rain of the night before had left treacherous hummocks, overflowing gutters and unexpected bogs of mud on highway and sidewalk alike.

The man was tall, lean and bare-headed, and he moved with a shoulder perpetually jutting against a wind that was not blowing, his hat swinging from one hand like an erratic propeller. Though he was obviously still young, his features had the final precision of statuary, as though mallet and chisel had done their last work. The woman presented a more indefinite picture, her outline blurred by a silver fox jacket, over the collar of which a blonde mop of hair flopped carelessly. It was evident that even without the bulkiness of the jacket she would be a little too plump for current standards. Yet there was nothing lurching nor awkward in her progress over the difficult footing. Rather, she negotiated these miniature Alps with the sure-footedness of a dancer, and though the man's hand always hovered gallantly near her elbow it was obvious she had no need of his assistance.

They were in no great hurry and they talked in trivial and easy irrelevancies, their glances resting with occasional incuriosity on the man now approaching them. By the brief case he carried and by his long strides he was obviously headed for a Boston train. Even though they were strangers in the neighborhood they were comfortably aware that here, as in most suburbs, there must be a 10:05 or a 10:17 or some such inevitable magic carpet for the late commuter. As he came abreast of them the woman was speaking. Her voice was high in pitch, yet it had some quality, some vibrant undertone that urged the ear pleasantly.

"Has the rain ruined all chance of fall color?" she was saying prosaically enough. "I've heard so much of the glorious New England autumn."

At the sound of her voice the commuter almost halted. His glance plunged directly into hers, not in the usual male quest, but in a sort of puzzled alertness. That glance held for only three seconds perhaps, then he gravely averted his look and passed them. Now they had the street entirely to themselves and they half-smiled at each other in recognition of the fact.

"You'll see plenty of color," the man promised. "Still September. It's only the late fall rains that can spoil the real show." She looked up at him with a little pleased nod.

A thoughtful onlooker, glancing from some near-by window might have thought: What extraordinary faces, so noble, so intent, so devoted. For these two leaned together from time to time almost involuntarily. Their glances sought each other, then moved away, then searched again. It was reasonable that this should be so, for they were bound by two firm ties. In the first place, they were man and wife. And secondly, they shared an even closer, more intimate relationship, the closest possible to mankind, perhaps. For each intended the death of the other and each had a suspicion of the other's intention. Or rather, not a suspicion, but a deep, primitive awareness.

The man paused, glanced at the number on a gatepost and shook his head. "This is it, the house must be up there beyond those trees. But it's a long driveway, Iris," he added ruefully, "and looks in even worse condition than this street. We should have taken a taxi after all."

"No, the air has been wonderful after those stuffy trains." She tasted the damp morning cold as a cat might taste some new delicacy, Taynor Harrison thought. Her eyes were like a cat's too, long and green, with infinitesimal pupils against the light. As they rounded a curve in the drive, the house came into view and she said, "You must have a lot of money, to afford a place like that, Tay." Her tone wasn't greedy. The words were merely a statement, as though she were a woman who made shrewd judgments and took it for granted that they should be confirmed. She went on without waiting for an answering comment.

"You still haven't told me how much of a household I'm going to meet."

"You haven't asked before," he said pleasantly. "The house agent promised cook, second maid and general man —but not before the end of the week. And that's the best they could do though it's a sizable place. The help problem's still pretty tough, you know. But Karen promised to see that the place was cleaned up and that there'd be groceries of a sort. We can make out alone, can't we, for a couple of days?"

"Of course. And I'm not a bad cook, though I haven't had my hand in for ages." She followed him up the steps and preceding him through the door he had unlocked, she stood looking around. In the entrance hall two huge Chinese vases held zinnias and chrysanthemums, and below a shallow flight of steps to their right a long living room spread in an easy and spacious informality. The bookshelves were still bare but on a table near by there was an array of the latest periodicals. A fire snapped in the grate.

Iris pulled off her hat and laughed.

"You're something of an Aladdin you know, to buy a place like this, sight unseen. And then find it waiting for you as though you'd lived in it forever."

"The home touches are Karen's," he reminded her. Iris descended the steps into the living room and paused, her hand on the delicate iron balustrade.

"You must tell me all about Karen before I meet her, Tay. I've been too tired and confused up to now to be curious about anything. I think I'm just coming alive again. But let's not answer other people's questions, darling. Let's just look mysterious and doting when they try to—pump us. Is that the right slang? Now that I'm actually in staid New England I shan't dare admit that I married you on a mere few days' acquaintance."

He was beside her now and his hand closed over hers. "I feel as though I had known you long before that, Iris. Long before."

"Another incarnation perhaps?" she asked lightly.

He nodded. "Another incarnation." And looked at her directly.

"Heavens, you make me feel creepy!" She disengaged her hand. "In fact, ever since we've landed in this home town of yours my bridegroom has been quite absent." She threatened him prettily. "So be careful or I shall vanish too. Now back to the questions. Karen, first. What's she like? Tell me all about her. All."

There was an almost comical look of dismay on his face. "Come to think of it, I can't tell you much of anything. I haven't seen her for nearly ten years. Let's look the house over first. The questions can wait. We'll have two whole days alone, you know, to get really acquainted with each other." He took her jacket as she shrugged herself out of it and added deliberately, "For me, at least, it will be like sitting down to a strange book that has had a—stimulating preface."

She smiled slowly and perhaps the downward glance of her eyes was as provocative as a flush. Taynor catalogued her charms with his own inward curl of the lip. Iris was really beautiful, he thought coolly. Even her plumpness was a soft, sensuous and fluid plumpness, the grace of her gestures and motions dictated by the slender arms and legs, rather than by the too full torso and hips.

"Then let's see the house," she said.

The house was mildly modern, owing its pleasantness to space and simplicity. If there was little originality in furnishings and architecture, at least there were charming vistas into still green gardens, rustic groves and a hedge-bound tennis court. In the middle of a busy suburb the place had privacy. All the rooms of the first floor were decorously as they should be: the living room, library, dining room, breakfast room, offices and kitchens. Paneling or tile, oriental rug or linoleum, everything was brisk and forthright, with no consoling imperfections. The previous owner had achieved that paradox, taste without imagination. In fact, for two people who had desperate need of impersonal small talk, perhaps there was too little on which to comment.

They turned to explore the upstairs regions. The third floor with its servants' quarters, game rooms and storage attics didn't hold them long. The second floor had several suites with possibilities of charm as yet undeveloped.

"With a little change of drapery and color?" Taynor suggested.

Iris nodded, then exclaimed,"Oh, but I like the master suite!" He stood aside to let her enter the large bedroom. From the doorway they could see the masculine dressing room, the chintz-paneled powder closet, the bath and the sleeping porch. But Taynor did not advance to examine any of these more closely. Instead, he stood frowning at the twin beds, which, hooked together and sharing the same coverlet, the same brocaded headboard, made a single Gargantuan couch.

"I don't know that I like these modern ideas," he said slowly. "We'd be more comfortable with separate rooms or at least, separate beds."

"But you have your own bed," Iris pointed out amiably. "It's simply that it's joined to the other, except when the maid does some extensive dusting. Quite chic. And sharing the marital couch is hardly a new idea, darling. It's thousands of years old!" As he still frowned, her hand touched his lapel, slid up about his shoulder, "We'll be together night and day," she teased, "you'll never get away from me."

Suddenly she relaxed in a complete abandonment and lay against him. For an instant he stood unresponsive, his arms at his side, staring beyond her with expressionless eyes. She lifted up her face so that the soft coral of her lips was near his. The man looked down at her then, with eyebrows sardonically arched. If his defeat was involuntary, at least it was acknowledged and self-contemptuous. His arms went around her, held her with a hard, peremptory roughness.

"You look like a mermaid," he said.

Iris didn't use make-up, and though there was never glow nor ebb of color beneath the creamy thickness of her skin, it was as smooth and poreless as a child's. Only in the pale pink of her lips, the pale green of her eyes, the pale gold of her hair and lashes was there color; pastel color, as something seen under water, shifting and indeterminate and elusive. He thought: Not using cosmetics is part of her secret. She never underlines anything about herself, as she might underline and emphasize her beauty if she wished. She is hard and definite inside, so the sheer instinct of self-preservation makes her camouflage and blur even her outer appearance. Well, his thought rushed on grimly, he was hard and definite himself.

His mouth obeyed the invitation of hers, touched her lips lightly, then with a seeking and bruising violence. This was the ultimate ugliness, he knew, to feel passion and repulsion simultaneously. Some would say it was the ultimate insanity. And he thought to himself quietly and without shock: Perhaps I am insane.

Iris said presently, "Let's see what we have in the larder. I should set about being very housewifely at once." Standing before a mirror she ran a comb through the disheveled blonde hair; but her glance at the reflection was careless.

Long ago she had studied the last footnote of her appearance and now found more novel mirrors in the eyes of others. Taynor did not follow her to the kitchen, but a few moments later he called to her from the front hall, a note of pleased excitement in his voice. "Come look, Iris, we missed one room! Down this way." A small foyer they had hurried by in their original tour gave entrance to still another room, it seemed. Taynor stood aside as she approached. "Music room," he said rather superfluously, for the Bechstein dominated the entire place. The cabinet victrola and radio, even the shrouded harp, were only modest satellites of the huge concert grand.

"This is a break, isn't it?" He smiled down at her. "You must sing for me. Often."

"But I don't—" She looked up at him, startled.

"Oh, come," his smile broadened, "I know a singing voice when I hear it speak!"

The rigid tenseness which had seized her as she stepped into the room relaxed a little. "M'Dieu, Tay, how did you know? Do I show my tonsils when I laugh? I thought you were an endocrinologist or something equally odd, not a throat specialist!"

"It was a good guess anyway, wasn't it?" he persisted. "You do sing."

"A little. It's not a trained voice. You'd be terribly disappointed." There was a little frown of puzzlement between her eyes as she stared around. Panels of brocade were set into the walls, a secluded alcove looked out into a dense and silent copse of firs. "It doesn't look like the rest of the house," she finally pronounced. "It's an odd shape—"

"For the acoustics, probably."

"Not just that. Even the decor is different. It has distinction. It wasn't planned by the same person." She crossed the room and knelt on the window seat, looking out. "I believe it's an addition, an afterthought. Look, it breaks the line of the original terrace."

"Well, a happy afterthought." Tay was affable as he threw the lid of the piano back. "Come on, sing something. Let's christen the room for us."

"Tay, not at this hour!"

"Why not? It isn't as though you had a smoker's croak in the morning." As she crossed behind him, obviously on her determined way toward the door, he whirled and caught one of her wrists lightly. "It's the first time I've asked you to do something special for me, Iris," he said.

She looked at him a moment, then her eyes veiled. Shrugging, she sat down on the piano bench and ran her hands over the keys. The tones were pure and authoritative and she looked up with a little air of surprise. "Concert pitch! It must have been tuned very recently." There was a sureness in her now, as though she had shaken off some feeling of unease as her hands touched the keyboard. Yet she repeated her warning. "My voice isn't trained, so I only attempt the light stuff. If you're an opera hound you'll have none of me."

"Go ahead." He stepped back from the piano, his hands behind him resting against the brocade that lined the paneled wall.

She hummed her way through *O What a Beautiful Morning* and then, rather surprisingly in view of her comment, launched into *Connais-tu le pays?* Her voice, effortless, naïve, true, held itself to the confines of the room, achieving an exquisite proportion to Tay's ear. The timbre was thrilling, on the thin edge of shrillness, yet held from it as a master's bow mutes the violin's stridency. On the semi-recitative the mezzo tones had a childish breathlessness infinitely appealing. Tay's eyes narrowed, then closed. He knew he was hearing a remarkable performance: trained vocal chords most perfectly imitating a young girl's immature yet potentially powerful voice. Even the last note was held an anxious fraction too long. Nice touch, that . . .

Her hands dropped from the keyboard and she looked up at him innocently. "I warned you."

"But it's a beautiful voice!" he exclaimed and hoped his tone held just the right touch of warm condescension. "And if that isn't opera, what is it? You must have lessons again. For you've had some surely, at least a few?"

"A long time ago when I was young," she said vaguely. Then she glanced up at him, her look kindling. "You know, now that we're back in America and really at home, we should celebrate. Let's shout *The Star-Spangled Banner!*"

Taynor's hand pressed against the piano until the ends of his fingers whitened. There was a soft roaring in his ears. "And I'm sure you could manage the high notes," he said finally, "but don't you think *Home, Sweet Home* would be more appropriate?" His tone was casual enough and he didn't look at her. There was a brief silence, then she rose from the bench and patted one palm, then the other with her handkerchief, in an unconscious, practised gesture.

"Enough singing for now," she said. "I'm sure it must be time for lunch. I'm hungry. I want my first meal in my first home."

They had a gay time in the kitchen, hunting pots and pans, giving confused orders, bumping into each other. Taynor had announced that lunch would be dinner this noon; they'd had such an early breakfast. They exclaimed over the crowded larder Karen had arranged.

"And what of Karen anyway? Our help and our deliverer and I know nothing about her!" Iris said as she tried to decipher the secrets of the electric stove.

Taynor had mixed them a cocktail apiece in celebration of the homecoming, and now he perched on the edge of the table and tasted his. "I told you I haven't seen her for ten years," he said. "She was about fifteen then. Sort of long and black and coltish."

"How do you mean, 'black'?"

"Her hair," he said vaguely. "It was all wild curls like an Australian bushman and she didn't know what to do with her arms and legs. But she was a nice youngster, what little I remember. Her mother and mine were close friends but of course I was ten years older so I didn't pay much attention to Karen, I'm afraid. She used to wait on me hand and foot, agog with awe because I was a budding medico. All young men are cads," he added comfortably.

"Fifteen," Iris said. "Then she must be twenty-five now. Twelve years younger than I am."

"You don't look thirty-seven."

"No." She accepted that without question, even without conceit, as though there were some vanity in her

stronger than the vanity of age-deception. "I look twenty-
seven, even in a strong light. But I didn't want to lie on
the marriage license and you mustn't give me away. Now
you," she went on thoughtfully, "you're thirty-five and
you look it, all of it. There's something about you that's
finished, forever and ever."

Taynor drained his glass. "But I don't want to be finished forever and ever," he protested with a grin. She
picked up her own glass for the first time and studied it.

"But that's the way you are. Finished. You should be
flattered."

"I bet you say that to all the boys." He quirked an eye-
brow and his teeth were a white flash in the tan of his face.

"What do you mean?" Her tone was a trifle sharp.

"Oh, it's just a slang phrase. You've been away from
American idiom too long, Iris."

"Oh. Well, here's to us." She waved her glass at him
and the sunlight refracted through it. "More about Karen,
please. How does it happen she's so willing to play the
good Samaritan and all that? After all, ten years is a long
time."

"She lost her mother too, shortly before I lost mine.
That was while I was overseas. I suppose she felt it made
some sort of bond between us, because our mothers had
been so close, you know. And she started writing me very
regularly. I'm an ungrateful hound," he admitted. "I
don't believe I answered more than one letter until I
knew I was coming home. Then it seemed very convenient indeed to know there was someone who'd contact
agents, buy a house for us, get everything ready and—well,
here we are, thanks to Karen." He looked a bit sheepish,

as though he had just now realized the extent of his debt.

Iris smiled. Her eyes were very green in the strong sunlight.

"I think I see her now," she said. "Someone very nice indeed, very efficient. Someone born to be used." Her contrite grimace was instant. "How horrid that sounded! I didn't mean it that way. I just meant"—she waved her hand about the kitchen—"all the nice, homey things she's done for us."

Tay stood up. "What's beside the chops and salad? Have you a keen hand with French-fried potatoes? Or, wait a minute—"

He strode to a closet door and flung it open. "How about rice? There must be some here. How long does it take to cook? Can't we have it instead of potatoes? You like rice, don't you?"

Iris set her unfinished glass on the drainboard. "Rice?"

"Yes. How about some with the chops? Of course, rice all by itself is a bit dull, but in its proper form, surrounded by chops and salad, it's a nice—change." He entered the closet and in a passable baritone began cajoling the crowded shelves, "Connais-tu le pays ou fleurit l' oranger?" Apparently the closet was complacent for he emerged still humming and flung a package of rice on a table. "Strictly speaking," he said cheerfully, "I should paraphrase by singing 'Dost thou know that fair land where the rice paddies blow?' What's the matter?" He looked at Iris apologetically. "Don't you like rice?"

Her smile moved only along the full upper lip which was an even paler coral than usual. "I like rice but I loathe parodies."

"Sorry." He was brisk. "From now on it's the land where the orange trees bloom, per usual." The music of her remembered singing still rose to his ears. Oddly and unbidden, the face of their chance-met commuter came to his mind, that passerby who, so many hours ago it seemed now, had almost halted at the sound of Iris' voice.

As it happened, the commuter had already forgotten both the voice and the encounter. He had made his train by a fraction of a second and he was now wholly absorbed at his desk in Boston. Iris and Taynor would never see him again. That they had seen him at all was merely due to the fact that as a disabled veteran, his employers were agreeable, for a time, to his commuting at hours generally considered more suitable for bankers and housewives than for clerks.

"Do we have rice or don't we?" Taynor said again, his hand on the package.

"It takes too long to cook."

He lit a cigarette and nodded. "I know. It's a bore waiting for rice. In my experience, it's generally a long, long wait."

The trivial words hung in the kitchen, as though they were almost visible in the motes of sunlight. Iris stabbed her cigarette through a smoke-ring hanging in that sunlight. "For such a quiet person you have a habit of making the most everyday remark sound portentous, Tay. I wish I knew you better."

"Oh, you will," he assured her. "You'll know me very well indeed before we're through."

They smiled at each other guardedly, pleasantly, like two fencers who circle on light and soundless feet.

2

THEY WERE OUT examining the rather unkempt tennis court the day two weeks later that Karen hailed them from the terrace. She ran forward to meet Taynor's outstretched hands but as he neared her, her run slowed to a walk as though the vanished ten years had suddenly become a formidable barrier. She shook hands almost shyly.

"You're here, Tay! Isn't it wonderful! And I'm so sorry all of us were at the Cape when you landed." Her wide smile faded though the warmth remained in her eyes. "But you're older, lots older," she added soberly, looking up at him. She didn't have to look far, for Karen was a tall girl. He put an arm around her shoulder and hugged her affectionately.

"You were here to do all the dirty work, Karen, and that was the kindest welcome home. You're a marvel and a raving tearing beauty too! That's what ten years did for *you*." He tucked her arm in his and led her toward Iris at a slow saunter. "That's a very magnanimous compliment, considering you've just accused me of premature old age."

"You know I didn't. I was just thinking that it was remarkable you could come out of that hell looking distinguished instead of—battered."

"Oh, I pick distinguished hells," he said airily. "Karen, I can't thank you enough for acting as my agent."

"Only liaison between you and the agents," she corrected. "Did the architect Dad suggested suit you?"

"It's a fine job."

She began hesitantly, "Tay, it's none of my business, but it seemed like so much money, the house and remodeling and everything."

He grinned. "There's always a psychological moment to dig into capital."

"You didn't!"

"It seems natural to see that horrified New England eye again," he commented. "Now I know I'm home. I gather you don't approve?"

"No."

"But I've been spending it for years."

"How could you, out there in the Pacific? And your mother only died last year."

"Not the capital she left me, my pet. My own. There're all kinds of capital besides money, you know," he teased.

She nodded gravely. "Health and nerves. Did you spend too much?"

"Listen to the babe in the wood! Iris, this is Karen Littlefield, dea ex machina."

Iris rose from the spectator bench and smiled her full limpid smile. "Saint Karen!" she said. "I refuse to call you Miss Littlefield. I presume Tay has thanked you for taking over the business headaches in connection with the house. But I'll wager he hasn't mentioned food or flowers or magazines or open fires or any of those things that made the place seem really home. It must have taken weeks of your time."

Karen looked back at Iris with eyes full of pleasure and

relief. "It wasn't anything," she said. "I was so glad to do it for Tay. And now I'm doubly glad if it gave you a pleasant homecoming too. It's good of you to say so because—" she hesitated "—well, most brides like to pick out their own homes themselves, don't they? But there were so few furnished houses available, even with the price latitude Tay gave me. You'll want to change a lot of things eventually, but at least the place is livable. Even if it is a bit—standardized."

It wasn't like Karen to chatter so volubly. But Tay had fallen into silence as the two women met, and even Iris' listening graciousness seemed as much engaged with his silence as with Karen's words. Perhaps it was always that way with a newly married couple, Karen thought doubtfully, but it did make one feel a bit outside of things. Even Tay suddenly seemed a total stranger. A pang of disappointment rose in her throat. Then Iris' easy gesture, motioning Karen to join her on the bench, dissolved that small fragmentary tension. Perhaps some small tension in Iris had dissolved too, while Karen was speaking.

"Do sit down. We'll have cocktails in a few minutes, if it's all right to offer them? But yes, even in America, unmarried girls of twenty-five should be allowed cocktails."

Karen laughed. "We're spinsters at that age. I gather you were not an American until you married Tay."

"But I am born American," Iris protested. "Only I have never seen New England before. These days I am just happy to sit and watch the leaves blow. I have never seen such red and gold and brown and scarlet. Is every New England September like this?"

"No, it's a very early fall," Karen said. "This is October

color really. We've been cheated of a warm month. Perhaps we'll have it later."

Iris laid a light hand on Karen's knee. "I saw a still-life once that I remember so well. A branch of just such autumn foliage lay on a table. A black velvet glove was tossed beside it. And a little in the background, a goblet half full of wine. Claret, it must have been, I think. Oh, the colors were so vivid, so contrasted, they struck one across the eyes! As though one had been blind to all color before."

Karen nodded. "I think I can see it. It must have been a gorgeous painting."

Iris' hand drifted back to her own lap. "It *was* gorgeous," she said. "I remembered it again when I saw you coming across the lawn. Your hair and eyes, so velvet black, the red and gold-brown of your skin. And the claret mouth."

The stain of rose deepened in Karen's tanned cheeks. But she said composedly enough, "Thank you," and no more. Evidently not one to fray a compliment to pieces, Iris thought coolly, and made a slight adjustment in an earlier judgment. But Tay, who had moved away to straighten a leaning tennis post, laughed aloud.

"You have something there, Iris. My wife," he said, brushing off his hands and coming toward them, "is apparently blessed with an artistic eye as well as musical talent."

"Oh, are you musical too?" Karen exclaimed with candid pleasure. "That's wonderful. Now perhaps you can drive Tay back to the piano again. Or at least make him start on his composing again. What do you do yourself? Play? Sing?"

Iris' hand reached out and snapped a leaf from a near-by bush. After a moment she said evenly, "I sing a little. As a matter of fact, you tell me something I didn't know, that my husband is a pianist." As she dissected the leaf her smile was rigid.

Karen said quickly, "He dislikes accompanying—"

"My ego suffers," Tay confirmed her solemnly.

"Since he is merciless with me I shall be merciless with him," Iris said. "If he insists I sing, he shall play for me."

Karen reproached Tay. "The beautiful Bechstein and a room 'specially for it, and you haven't been playing! Not in two whole weeks? Why, Mrs. Harrison, Tay could have been a concert pianist. He actually was one for a year."

Tay said, "Why didn't you give me time? I was going to wait until Iris was thoroughly bored with me, and then smite her all of a heap with my master talent. But now that you've ruined my big moment, Karen, I shall just sulk and play *To a Wild Rose* four times a day."

Karen's laughter was contrite. "I'm sorry if I put my foot in it." She added simply, "I guess I took it for granted that married people knew every last thing about each other."

"Darling, you're priceless." Iris was amused. "Married people know the *last* thing about each other, but very seldom the things that led up to the last thing!"

"Riddles, riddles," Tay objected. "Speaking of riddles, Karen, j'accuse. There was a long time when I didn't hear from you. Why not? And I won't be put off with the very excellent retort that I didn't answer your letters at all, until I was on my way home. And then only to ask further favors. You coddled my maharajah complex and it's all your own fault. Did you get thee to a nunnery during that time?"

"Not exactly. I was in Africa and Sicily with an ambulance unit. Driver. Sort of busy at first and a bit crocked later."

"Ill? Wounded?"

Karen looked sheepish. "Ambulance-jeep collision," she mumbled. "The jeep won. I was thrown out on my head. Fractured my right arm and had a rather mean concussion too." Suddenly her mouth worked, then broke into harlequin mirth, her white teeth gleaming in the vivid small triangle of her face. "Department of irony: When I came to, I found my three passengers had risen from their stretchers and carried me to the field hospital!" She laughed a little jerkily.

Iris stood up and put a slim hand on Karen's shoulder. "Such a long time ago." Her smooth voice pulled them back to the serenity of a suburban afternoon. "The war's over. Let's have those cocktails. Tay shall play for us while we imbibe—since he won't join us. For some reason he is inflicting a spell of austerity on himself."

"It's the most unrewarding of vices," Tay said lazily as they strolled toward the house. Karen glanced up at him.

"But you never drank much."

"Austerity, I mean, not alcohol. Now sloth, there is much to be said for sloth. No, I never drank much except for occasional binges. I shall drink again sometime and still—not much. But there are times in life when one suf-

fers, or enjoys, a schizophrenic phase." He squeezed Iris'
elbow. "Split personality to you, Mrs. Harrison. During
such a time one walks delicately like Agag, and doesn't try
to merge the two egos with the alcoholic link."

Karen laughed. "Don't you want to merge them?"

"Merge them? Perish the thought. I hope to keep them
permanently apart until one or the other is destroyed."
He stood on the lower step of the terrace now, looking up
at her. The sunlight struck warmly against his tanned
cheeks, the crisp hair that was scarcely lighter. Between
the deep brackets of the two lines that carved his face his
smile was wide for the first time, revealing the rows of
strong white teeth. For an instant that smile gave his
youth back to Karen; or would have if the eyes above it
had not remained aloof, having no part in the smile.

Iris said petulantly, "Perhaps you will make better sense
at the piano."

He played Chopin's *Fantasie Impromptu,* and from the
first note the two women sat in bemused silence, their
glasses untouched. When he had finished Karen picked up
her cocktail, sipped it. "You still are, Tay, you still
are . . ."

"Though a bit of Hanon is indicated, eh?"

She smiled. "Naturally, after all this time. I remember
when you wouldn't perform if you'd missed two consecu-
tive days of practice. Tay, what's the theme there that's
so familiar?"

He stood up, flexing his fingers. *"I'm Always Chasing
Rainbows.* Lifted lock, stock and barrel from friend
Chopin." Iris had sat in silence, making no comment

whatsoever on Tay's performance. Now she said, "Chasing rainbows, what a dull pursuit."

Karen stood up. "But easy on the eyes."

"And don't forget the pot of gold," Tay pointed out. "That's definite enough even for a pragmatist like you, Iris."

Iris yawned, emphasizing her boredom. She turned to Karen politely. "I am sure the shaker holds another dividend."

"Mercy, no. It's too late. And I've forgotten the main reason I dropped in. Dad wants you to have dinner with us tomorrow night. Can you?"

"We'd love it."

"Have you a car yet, Tay, or shall I call for you?"

"We'll taxi."

"You'll be able to wangle a car all right as soon as you start practice. Doctors rate."

Taynor said, "I'm not sure when I'll start practice again. Or if I ever will."

"But Tay—" Karen fell silent. One gaff to an afternoon was enough, she thought ruefully. It was always her failing that when she liked people her enthusiasm and concern ran far ahead of her decorum. These, after all, were two strangers. Even the bond she had always thought of as existing between herself and Tay was probably existent only in her own mind. That she had hero-worshiped once, that she had been able to do a little service for him recently, was no excuse for being an amiable meddler now, she admonished herself sternly.

They went with her to the car, then walked slowly back to the house. Still adjusting her gloves, Karen glanced over her shoulder at them. They were standing motionless now, their heads slightly inclined toward each other. The late afternoon sun refracted from a window and enclosed the two figures in a cold globe of light. It was as though they were insulated in some alien and soundless medium, not only from her, but from all the world she knew. Karen shivered a little and started the motor. The afternoon was growing chilly.

Tay said, "I was quite taken with your description of Karen. Was there really ever a painting like that, or did you make it up on the spur of the moment?"

"There was such a painting," Iris said, and added indifferently, "A pity no one ever told Karen that a large mouth shouldn't be smothered in blood-red lipstick. Do all girls her age look like careless Columbines? I see I shall have to learn my America all over again."

Tay held the door open for her. "And what part of it *is* your America?" he asked gently.

"Oh, stop being cryptic!" she snapped. For the first time she allowed her composure to be shaken visibly. She walked into the living room and picked up the shaker from the small portable bar. She poured herself a drink and stood looking at him, her lips in a thin hard line. "It's annoying and frightfully sophomoric to answer every question with a question. And to underline nearly every remark you deign to make as though it were the utterance of an oracle! Sometimes I could scream. It's like wearing away stone with drops of water!" She attempted to smile, drained her glass and refilled it. "Sure you don't want one?" He shook his head.

She said more quietly, "I suppose all married people

have little habits that get on each other's nerves. But when we first met you didn't have that peculiar mannerism."

"This is all news to me." He was unperturbed.

She emptied the second glass, set it down and then came over to perch on the arm of his chair. She leaned against him so that one soft breast pressed his shoulder. "I'm sorry I was so cross. Trouble is, Tay, we don't know enough about each other. Oh, I realize we had a sort of tacit understanding that we'd start life together without digging into each other's pasts."

"It wasn't tacit. You suggested it."

"I know. I thought it would be fun being mysterious for a while. But it won't be fun much longer. This afternoon I felt like a perfect idiot not knowing that you were a pianist, a professional."

He patted her hand. "It will indeed be the day when you're a perfect idiot."

"Merci. But let's make a new start, shall we? Tell all? It's quite brave of me"—her lips wore a rueful smile —"because it's bad enough being older than you without your discovering my terribly uninteresting past. After all, the only advantage an older woman has over young girls is—mystery. But even if I toss my aces away, it will be worth it if you promise not to like me less."

"I couldn't like you less," he said positively. One of the gilt locks that framed her face had fallen forward in juxtaposition to his hand. And now he tugged at it playfully. "One thing, of course, is impossible. No beautiful woman can have had thirty-seven uninteresting years. Or twenty-three, shall we say? I suppose we must concede that you were once a child. Or were you?"

"You really think I'm beautiful, Tay?"

"I really do. Don't I show it?"

"Only—at times." She rose and stood looking at him. "Let's bargain. You catalogue everything you know about me and I'll fill in the omissions. Then we'll start on you. It's very unfair," she laughed, "because I've had three cocktails and you've had none. But I'm game. Your turn first."

Tay made a tent of his fingers. "Well," he said slowly, "you were born in California but you spent all your school years in France and India. Your father's business was oriental antiques, wasn't it? Your mother died when you were three. There was a silly school-girl elopement in Paris when you were sixteen—and an annulment. Seven years ago you married a British major who was killed in the Shanghai massacres. Due to his army duties, however, you hadn't seen him for two years before his death. Through friends of his you finally managed to wangle your way from India to Lisbon where you hoped to take off for America." He paused. "You had passport trouble there because your father was dead, your British husband was dead and you had difficulty proving your American birth."

Tay looked up, planted his hands in a more relaxed position on the arm of his chair and grinned broadly. "There in Lisbon a certain Colonel Harrison finally caught up with you—"

"Caught up with me?"

"I think I must have been looking for you for years—if you'll forgive my being sophomoric again," Tay said. "You were the girl of my dreams. At any rate, this Har-

rison chap pulled a few strings, married the chic but dis-
mal damsel and brought her home to a chilly New England fall."

Iris clapped her hands. "But, Tay, you know *every*
thing about me! I shall hardly have to fill in at all." She
put her head to one side. "But how did you find out about
that first marriage? I suppose I should feel ashamed, yet
it's so long ago it seems to have happened to a different
person. Honestly, I doubt if I'd have thought to mention
it to you. How did you know?" she repeated.

"Oh, these days all kinds of dossiers have to be consulted
before even such a simple thing as marriage between two
Americans can take place—abroad," Tay said vaguely. "It
confused things rather, a French and then a British husband. The American consulate and I had to follow all
sorts of trails."

Iris said interestedly, "But it's amazing! Do you mean
Lisbon and Paris and Bombay actually kept records about
a poor little mouse like me?"

"Marriages and passports all mean records. You certainly should be glad of the French one, that showed you
were born here. Otherwise, I might have had some difficulty in—well, collecting you. Now let's fill in the inter-
ludes. Why was there an annulment of the French
marriage?"

"Because I was too young. He was my singing teacher
and at least fifty. Disgusting, hein? But he convinced me
in eight short lessons that my voice would be a world's
wonder—"

"It is."

"—and I married him out of sheer gratitude. It lasted

not two days, until papa found us. I can't remember a
thing about him, my first husband I mean, except that he
had beautiful black hair and mustaches. I've hated black
hair ever since. Poor Jules."

"And the years between sixteen and thirty?"

"They were lovely." Iris was ecstatic. "Simla during
the heat, and little trips with papa. Nothing that a man
would find very exciting, of course. The usual things
young girls are allowed in India."

"There were three years between your father's death
and your marriage to Major Terence O'Hearn," Tay suggested.

"Everyone was so lovely." Her voice was vague, sor-
rowful. "I just kept on living the same way, not realizing
papa had left so little. Then Terry came along."

"But couldn't be with you much."

"No. Don't think me shallow, but even life with Terry
seems a bit dreamlike now. You see, almost at once he
was being sent here and there, to Singapore and Shanghai
and places. At first I went with him, but after a while it
was simpler just to keep our home in India and wait for
him to come back to me when he could."

"You had your singing at least." Tay was sympathetic.

"Oh, I'd given that up long ago. I fear I just settled
down to the usual routine of gossip, teas—oh, all the foreign colony frivolity. Almost grass widow, as you would
say. It wasn't very good," she pronounced with an air of
frankness. "You know what I mean, Tay? But don't
blame me too much. Just be sweet enough to skip over
those years and not peer into them too much. Label it
my silly era in capital letters, period. When I heard of

Terry's death, it jolted me back to normalcy with a vengeance!"

"But you didn't hear of his death until almost two years
after it happened," he observed mildly.

She stared at him. "How did you—? Oh, of course.
You had that from my dear friend, the Comtesse, in Lisbon! Well, I *wasn't* at home when Terry died, they
couldn't find me nor get word to me." Slow tears touched
her lashes, but the eyes were as clear green as ever. "I told
you it was my silly era, didn't I?" She hesitated, stared at
him, plunged on. "It was a Utopia I thought I had found,
but it was false, false! I regret it, but I do not blame myself
too much. And you are tolerant, I think, I know. I was
so lonely and I thought myself at last in love. And finally,
there was escape from the hateful war—all away from the
world, a dream place." She paused for breath.

"Shrangri-la, no doubt."

"That isn't amusing. You disappoint me."

"I'm not amused."

"Then why are you smiling? Are you trying to egg me
into telling you where I was, who he was?"

"God forbid. Who started this foray into Truth and
Consequences, anyway?" Tay filled his pipe.

She relaxed, stretched her arms, smiled. "Do I sound
terribly promiscuous?"

He shook his head. "Patient." Her hand hesitated over
the cocktail shaker, dropped away. She sat down. His
smile widened. "You can hold your liquor too, Iris, know
when to stop."

"Not always. You've seen me—stimulated."

"At your own choice." He flipped the match expertly

into the tray behind him. "I wouldn't say your failings were either liquor or men."

"What are they?"

"How should I know? Money? Power, perhaps?"

Her laugh rang gaily now and she curled up on the couch looking like a plump small kitten. "Well, if it's money, I've done very well, apparently." She looked about the room. "But if it's power I've been born centuries too late. Not many modern women want power, Tay. They just want peace and security."

"So does a boa constrictor after a substantial meal," Tay offered goodhumoredly. She laughed again.

"Sometimes you are most comical. Now it's my turn about you. You were throwing a gorgeous party in Lisbon and I was invited to it through a friend of a friend of yours. And I came very timidly and you were wonderfully sweet to me. And that's how it happened between us. But before that"—Iris in her turn raised her hands and ticked the small facts off upon each finger—"you were born here and you went to Exeter, Harvard and medical school. Later you studied abroad. You were an only child and you have been left quite a bit of money that hasn't spoiled you—except that you are taking much too long a vacation, honeymoon or not." Her tone held mock rebuke. "The war broke out and you enlisted. Where was that, in England or France?" She broke off, then waved a hand. "Never mind. Let me finish what I know, then you can fill in. You were captured and spent a long time in an Italian concentration camp in Africa. You were royally making up for that time when I met you in Lisbon."

She paused, lit a cigarette and stretched her legs luxuriously. "You were throwing the party of a century," she
went on, "you were stately, you were eligible, you were
single. You were also drunk as a lord. For some strange
reason you picked me out from forty women, most of them
much younger—"

"None half as interesting—"

"And proposed to me a very few days later. When you
were sober, I'm thankful to remember." She threw her
head back and laughed richly. "Now, how wrong am I?
Are there any corrections or additions?"

"Only about the camp part. I can't imagine where you
gathered the notion I served in Africa."

"The Comtesse said so."

He shook his head. "But you and I agreed to ignore
any communiqué issued by the Comtesse, didn't we? No.
I had just landed in Lisbon the week before I met you.
Suez route from the Pacific."

"Then you weren't a prisoner of war?"

"That? Oh, yes, yes." He tapped the ashes from his
pipe. "But not in Africa. My service was in the Pacific,
I was in a Jap prison camp."

Ester appeared just inside the archway with the usual
mumbled ritual and he stood up. "Have to postpone the
rest. Are you hungry? I am." He took Iris' hand, pulled
her from the couch, shook her playfully as Ester vanished.
"If you hurry, you can finish the shaker."

Her fingers touched her hair uncertainly. But there was
nothing uncertain in her voice. "I've had enough," she
said. "I have had quite enough."

3

Apparently here in New England there was no tradition that the males should sit over the port. Iris felt a vague disappointment for she had counted on some intimate conversation with Karen. Karen puzzled her and Iris didn't enjoy being puzzled. As things stood she had had little choice as far as Tay was concerned. If her recent cobweb suspicions of him were confirmed she would have to take a further and final risk, but that still lay in the future and perhaps it would not be necessary. She preferred not to think of it until or unless it was forced upon her. Sometimes there was no alternative but physical violence, but Iris shrank from it as fastidiously as she had shuddered from washing dishes those two days until the servants had arrived. Tay had done kitchen police.

But Karen . . . Iris was anxious to place her. It was important to make no mistake there. Karen was young but she wasn't gauche, she was candid but she had discernment. She was, Iris judged with a little inner shrug, virginal, but she must have learned much of men in her experience overseas. Normally she had a vast zest for life —you couldn't mistake those who carried that inner banner—but at the moment she was obviously high-strung, unable to settle down either to a business routine or a social domesticity. In America, it must apparently be one thing or the other for an unmarried girl. Hideously dull.

American parents did these things badly. They filled

their daughters with half-baked and idealistic ideas about
men, frowned upon their consorting with an older age-
group. Yet how was a girl to find an eligible parti among
these tennis-playing young men who still had their way
to make in the business world? And now with war casual-
ties, there would be fewer even of these ineligibles. Iris
caught her breath, then with the ease born of practice,
sent that thought scurrying away on tiny, micelike feet.

Someone had turned on the news hour as they returned
from the dining room, so she could sit back silently and
let her casual glance rest first on one or the other of the
Littlefields. There were only three of them, Karen, her
brother and her father, for Judge Littlefield was a wid-
ower. He was a tall, dark-skinned man in his fifties, with
a shock of close-cropped gray hair; and an easy, unassum-
ing manner that hid, she didn't doubt, a good deal of
native shrewdness. She was relieved to feel sure that he
had liked her instantly. Most men did. She had also been
amused during dinner to notice how often he glanced
from her to Karen as though just realizing how much
make-up his daughter used. The masculine mind was still
apt to accept an unpainted face as synonymous with virtue;
a very useful assumption she had found. And if once Tay's
quizzical comment had proved him an exception it merely
established the general rule.

Now that Karen's brother Gregory was sitting down she
found no discomfort in looking at him for his crippled
leg was not noticeable except when he walked. Even then
his limp wasn't too marked but it annoyed her. Though
she had seen literally thousands of much worse deformities
she still felt repelled by any physical imperfection. It

roused something cruel in her as though it were a deep
outrage committed against her personally. She remembered how when she was a small child she had come upon
two tiny birds that had fallen from their nest. She had
allowed the one that was whole to hop into the underbrush. But the nestling that had a broken leg—she had
stamped upon it again and again in a sort of blind involuntary fury. No one had seen that act.

She had not been so fortunate that time in India when
she was seventeen, the time she had kicked the mutilated
beggar over whom she had stumbled. That episode had
had messy repercussions and for quite a time thereafter
she had traveled with her father because the foreign colony
had turned a cold shoulder. Those beggars had horrible
and weird diseases and it was dangerous to touch them,
even with a foot. She rubbed her slipper against the soft
pile of the rug and smiled gently at Gregory. He must
resemble his mother for he was light-haired and stocky,
unlike his sister and father. An extremely good-looking
chap too, if one could forget his leg. Twenty-eight?
Twenty-nine? Hardly younger than that though his face
had a strange innocence that had nothing to do with in-
experience. Iris was familar with that look. It was worn
by those who offer themselves to pain again and again
without fighting it. Inevitably one struck at such faces for
the faces themselves had chosen that destiny, not the hands
that struck. The faces, in fact, should apologize to the
hands. If an argument were unsound one didn't blame
the conclusion; one blamed the premises, as Iris' father
had often pointed out.

She missed her father at times, she thought with a mild

surprise. A pity that he had had to be left with only that
old fool to nurse him; and no money because Iris had had
greater need of it. But if he had been conscious on his
deathbed he would have seen the logic of his daughter's
apparent desertion, the unquestionable logic.

Her thoughts drifted, washing as seaweed washes, slith-
ering from this thought or wrapping a tentacle about that;
but always borne on the tide of her remorseless rhythm
and sureness. The seaweed came to a momentary rest and
she turned to Gregory. "Are you following in your father's footsteps and studying law?" He shook his head.

"No. I was first-year medical when I was drafted and
I'm going ahead with it now. A year or two later in the
game and they wouldn't have taken me at all; they re-
versed the policy. But I'm not sorry," he added cheerfully, "I wouldn't have missed the show for anything. And
now I know what I'm headed for eventually, plastic surgery. Listen, Tay isn't really going to quit practice, is he?
Karen wasn't sure whether he was joking or not, but she
was quite panicky."

Iris smoothed a creamy satin fold of her dress. "We
haven't discussed it at all. But it doesn't matter much one
way or another, does it? Tay seems to have enough to be
comfortable." Her cheeks lifted in a mischievous smile.
"And frankly I do think he picked a thoroughly dull
specialty. Endocrinology. Now plastic surgery, that's exciting. What a thrill to make people all over again, in
front of one's very eyes!"

"Endocrinology makes 'em all over again, too," Gregory
said.

"But not so quickly, so spectacularly as plastic surgery

does. For a time at least," she added reflectively, "I should think you would feel like God, or as God would feel if he existed."

Gregory threw an arm over the couch and turned toward her more fully, his look on her eyelids which, when she was glancing down, were like semicircles of cream. "Atheist?"

"Agnostic, rather. For that matter, I've lived in India so long that at times I can see a certain amount of sense in animism."

"A highly evolved specimen like you attracted by the most primitive form of religion?"

"All religion is primitive to the adult mind, isn't it?" she asked lightly. "We're put here as the tiger or the house fly are put here, to struggle, fight and survive during our life cycle. Or to struggle, fight and die, prematurely. That being the case, the first law of life is power, isn't it? A word that contradicts most religions."

Judge Littlefield's voice spoke behind them, quietly. "The word sounds a bit ruthless in the sense you're implying, Mrs. Harrison; that is, if you're denying the compulsion of religious or ethical restraints." The words were didactic but his tone was amused, light. He passed the arm of the couch and seated himself facing her. "By its very essence power can't be static. It must be used on or against something or someone."

"Or for something or someone, Dad."

"But of course." Iris' eyes were bright and very clear as she looked at Judge Littlefield. His amusement had annoyed her. "And to challenge religion isn't to deny ethics, is it? But I defend my statement that power is the first law of existence. If your son becomes a plastic surgeon he will be expressing his personal power very definitely even though constructively. A molder of men. And you yourself as lawyer and judge, you must have tasted power very often." She added slowly, "Personal power."

"A judge is merely the interpreter of impersonal law and justice." He was imperturbable.

Iris picked up her liqueur glass. "The important word there is 'interpreter.' In the last analysis, it is your own personal interpretation of the law, your own bent or bias, shall we say, that determines any issue brought before you."

"Or the jury's bent or bias," he said dryly.

She nodded. "Of course. The jury is powerful too." Her face kindled. "Do women serve on juries in this state? I've always wanted to serve on a jury."

Judge Littlefield smiled. "Women don't serve, not here. But they are fighting for that somewhat dubious privilege. I needn't ask in what field you exert your power, Mrs. Harrison. Beauty guides with a single hair while the rest of us struggle with towlines. We can only be grateful that since you hold such a dangerous doctrine"—he hesitated and picked his phrasing gallantly—"at least your weapons against us are traditional."

"And obvious?" she smiled. He glanced at her with a sharpened interest, stood up.

"I see that Karen and Tay are having a turn in the garden," he said. "How about joining them? It's a full moon and so warm I don't believe you'll need a wrap. Come along, Greg?"

But Gregory shook his head. When they had stepped

through the French window he raised himself from the
couch and limped across the room to watch them descend
the terraces. The moonlight merged Iris' gown and hair
into a single pale aura. Gregory switched off the near-by
lamp and let his own face lift to the sky glory. To this
small degree he was sharing the night with her. It was all
he hoped to share, ever. It would be enough to be with
her occasionally, to see her soft maternal figure moving
gracefully about this room. Maternal? His breath caught
suddenly. When Iris had leaned forward to accept a cigarette light, her low-cut gown had given him an intimate
glimpse of a very full but somehow very unmaternal
breast. For a moment he had cynically presumed that the
generosity was intentional; an instant later he had been
thoroughly ashamed of himself.

For Iris had lifted her eyes to his as the light flared between them. They were such pure green eyes, as cool and
clear as brook water with the lovely spread of smooth white
forehead above them. Those eyes had gravely held and
abashed his thought, a thought that would never recur.
For Iris was as honest as her eyes, with a funny brave little
honesty. How many women would have professed so can-
didly such a philosophy, in a world that had sickened and
nearly died of its ugliness? Yet it was obvious that she
believed it, just as it was equally obvious that she didn't
live by it, that such a woman *couldn't* live by it. Gregory's
lips wore a line of gentle amusement. Then he scowled.

He wished he had expressed himself as honestly, that he
had declared his own deeply contrary convictions. But he
had hesitated under her look, for some cowardly reason
reluctant to be accused either of naïveté or idealism, which

for a moment he had thought synonymous to Iris. While
he had hesitated, his father had spoken and the moment
had passed. Gregory sighed. And Peter denied the Lord,
he thought wryly. It proved again that he had been right
in giving up theology and going into medicine instead.

The butler, moving silently about the room collecting
coffee cups and liqueur glasses, glanced at Gregory. The
moonlight had washed the lines of weariness and pain
from his face. It looked very young. There was resigna-
tion there but no defeat; and some inner radiance too, if
one could use such a phrase in describing a stocky young
man with a lame leg.

There was a late-summer feel in the air, here in the cup
of the lowest garden. The asters were shorn of color by
the steel edge of the moonlight and the smoke of Taynor's
pipe curled across them in miniature halos that hovered,
then drifted away. The poplars around the garden were
black clouds, except where their crowns silvered to the
sky. Karen said again desperately, "But I can't understand
you, Tay. You cared so much for your profession. And
you're too young to retire. You're fully recovered now,
you said so in your letter. You've had months out of the
hospital to racket around and—how was it you put it?—to
'see a damaged world from an even gloomier civilian view.'
Perhaps if you went back to your work the view wouldn't
look quite so gloomy."

"It's a nice clarion call but I can't seem to gallop."

"Is it—" she hesitated, corrected herself. "Perhaps Iris
wants to travel some more?"

"I don't know what Iris wants to do. I only know that
I no longer feel equipped to go on with medicine."

"But that's ridiculous. All you need is some refresher work."

Tay said gently. "You're not ingenuous, really."

Karen looked up at him from the bench where she sat. From her too the moon had washed away the vivid color so that her face seemed all huge black eyes and wide mouth, grape-dark. "No," she said, "I'm not ingenuous. I suppose I found it easier to grapple with a surface argument. What you've really been telling me is that somewhere along the line you've lost faith in yourself. No, not in your ability to practice competently, I understand that, but something deeper. Some warmth, some eagerness, some spark." She waited but he was still silent and she went on.

"You're not unique, Tay. All over the world now there are millions of similar cases. Perhaps it could be called a sort of combat fatigue of the soul."

He emptied his pipe and sat down beside her. "Suffering a bit from it yourself, aren't you?"

"Yes," she said gravely, "that's why I envy you."

"Envy me?"

"You have your work, your profession. You have something to keep your mind and your hands busy while—" She groped for a phrase.

"While the ego is convalescing?"

She nodded again. "But I have nothing, no talent, no profession. For a little while I found something useful to do there in Africa. Now I'm a parasite again. That's why I envy you."

"You'll find something eventually."

"Of course. I'm healthy and young and one of these

days I'll wake up and start exploding with energy once more. My circumstances are just what they were before the war and I'm sure I bubbled over with ideas and plans in those days. Trouble is, none of them were definite or urgent—and now I've forgotten even what they were." She swung her feet thoughtfully. "Tay, you're one of the fortunates. You know, a lot of us are walking from a rather demolished world into a big, still undamaged room where there are all sorts of tools and instruments. But we're lost, we don't know what to do with them. We never learned them, you see. But you do know. The undamaged room is waiting for you. You can go directly to a certain bench, pick up certain tools. They're familar to your hands. You can set about your work again almost automatically, no matter how you feel inside."

"And you?"

She smiled a little wanly. "Oh, I'm just looking around, picking up one thing, then another. And all of them strange to me. About the only thing I can do at the moment is kibitz on the fortunate ones like you."

He said teasingly, "I've caught you out in one vice. You're a born impresario."

She laughed outright. "A born meddler, you mean! I know it. It's just that if one is fated to stand on the sidelines it's unbearable to see the actual players refuse to perform. I suppose it's an itch to be part of the game somehow, even if I'm only rated as nuisance value. And you'll notice," she added cheerfully, "another of my besetting sins, mixing metaphors. Like the man who broke the ice and found himself in hot water." She looked up.

"Isn't that Mrs. Harrison and Dad on the first terrace? She's very lovely, Tay."

"She asked you to call her Iris." He went on irrelevantly, "I'm pleased with the house, Karen. Your magic wand did a yeoman's job."

"The best part of the house is the music room, and you arranged for all that yourself."

His voice held a trace of embarrassment. "You had done so much as it was. I didn't want you to feel any responsibility at all if the room didn't suit me. That's why I sent the specifications directly to the architect."

"That was thoughtful." She dimpled. "As a matter of fact, though you don't know it, that room added quite a bit of zest to our lives for a time."

"Yes?" He stirred and crossed his legs.

"Dad and I wandered over one day to see how the work was progressing. And Tay, the contractor wouldn't let us in!"

Tay said with an air of vast surprise, "Why on earth not?"

"Now I *am* disappointed! Dad was right, then. He said the contractor evidently confused his orders and was being ultra-cautious. But of course Greg and I wouldn't accept anything as simple as that. We immediately dubbed it the Mystery Room and offered two theories. The tamer one was that you were going seriously into concert work and were dedicating the room to your sacred art, that no alien foot must ever contaminate the precincts, you know. And that theory is already exploded."

"And the other?"

"Greg favored that one because he has a weakness for

Gilbert and Sullivan, particularly *The Mikado*. We decided that when you escaped from the Jap camp you captured Yum-yum and Pitti-sing singlehanded and à la
Superman," Karen laughed, as she rambled on, swinging
her feet idly. "And you sent the two wenches home in that
large crate—it couldn't have held anything as prosaic as a
grand piano! Once here they'd be decanted into the music
room and fed exclusively on a diet of music, to make the
punishment fit the crime, you know!"

Tay uttered a short sound that might have been a laugh.
Karen sat up and said interestedly, "That gives me an
idea, a serious one. *Bluebeard* would make a wonderful
libretto, with ballet perhaps. Has it ever been done?
Why don't you take a whirl at a score for it?"

Tay stood up as Iris and Judge Littlefield started across
the plot toward them, moving slowly down the flagstone
path among the autumn roses. His foot must have been
asleep, for he stumbled a little as he rose. "Why don't *you*
take up writing? You're quite a romancer, Karen." The
stumble may have twisted his ankle, for his tone was almost sharp. "Oh, by the way," he added, "I'd appreciate
it if you folks didn't let on to Iris that I had the music
room built specially. She's the thrifty one in the family
and I'm afraid it would spoil her pleasure if she knew it
was an added extravagance on my part."

"Of course. I'll speak to Dad and Greg about it."
Karen's voice was flat. For a long half-hour there had been
an easy, warm companionship between them. Now she
had bored him, she thought ruefully. Perhaps he had
even tagged her as that repulsive object, a whimsey-
perpetrator. Or again, it may simply have been Iris' ap-

proach that had changed his manner. That alternative
thought was a relief. Tay had always been unswerving in
his single-mindedness. Young as he was, his devotion to
his profession had already given him standing; and even
in his avocation, music, his brilliance had been notable.
Now it was to his marriage, no doubt, that he was bending
all his mind, his present eagerness. Probably he was honestly unaware of anyone's else existence when his wife
was near.

It must be wonderful to be so much in love. Karen felt
a warm rush of gratitude toward Iris. Tay would be com-
pletely healed soon, living in that atmosphere of affection.
She wouldn't meddle any more. It was Iris' privilege, not
hers, to see that Tay went back to his profession; and the
matter could safely be left to Iris' soft, persuasive hands.

Karen could see those hands in her mind's eye, though
not in the dimming moonlight. Iris moved her hands seldom, but when she did, her gestures were purposeful.

Gregory said diffidently, "Karen has supplied me with a good excuse, a message for you, Iris. I wanted to come over anyway." He halted on the threshold where Ester had left him, and squinted against the afternoon sunlight. Iris tossed her fashion magazine aside and motioned him to one of the rustic terrace chairs.

"Oh, nice to see you, Greg. Now I have an excuse for loafing, too, though these warm fall days hardly need any excuse, do they? I'm used to a lot of heat and sunlight, and Tay has warned that I'd better lay in a supply before your New England winter sets in."

"I hope it will be your New England, too, presently."

"Oh it will," she assured him lightly. "I adapt to new places and people very easily."

She would too, he thought. People who traveled in their minds always did. There was about her something swift and transient, as though her inner eye were never set on immediacy. She wouldn't settle into some hard unchanging mold. Even her physical appearance seemed to vary, judging by the dozen times he had seen her. In this sunlight as in moonlight or lamplight, her exquisite skin was as challenging as ever. Yet Gregory for the first time revised his estimate of her age. She was nearer his years than Karen's, he decided, possibly even a year or two older than he. It may have been the tailored suit she wore, for Iris wasn't the tailored type. Though it wasn't possible for her to be plain, this was certainly one of her older, less glowing days.

Gregory was glad that he could see her so. In some way it seemed to advance his knowledge of her and paradoxically it added a new, protective element to what he had assured himself jeeringly was a calf-love infatuation. If he had felt anything—well, unappealing about Iris, it had been her apparent immunity to the passions, the gropings of the convulsive world around her; as though she had been born with a shell translucent but impervious, while most of her contemporaries still wore raw and quivering skins. Now he could see her immunity as qualified. She was subject to the common human denominator, the encroachment of the years. A part of Gregory that had been questioning, hesitant, dissolved into tenderness. It would be a decade before her beauty would begin to blur, but he wished passionately that he could fend her from even the knowledge of those coming years.

It was different with him, of course. In some ways he had been born old, he reflected. Even as a small boy, some intuitive sense, some preview of the future had always overleaped his calendar years; so that at ten he had guessed the uncertainties of adolescence, so that now at twenty-eight he had already tasted middle age and compromised with it.

"What's amusing you?" Iris asked.

"I was thinking what a coward I am," he said cheerfully, "such a coward that I anticipate pangs before they happen, like the White Queen. But it's not a bad system, you know."

Her smile was lazy. "What pang do you anticipate now?"

"Oh, I anticipate happiness as well as pangs." He was prompt. "And speaking of anticipation, I'm rather hoping you'll sing for me, now." As he saw her frown, he went on quickly, "I know you won't sing after dinner and that you prefer not to sing in the morning. But now, at four o'clock? Tay said it was a good time to catch you."

"Tay loves to catalogue people and their habits," she said in a very unbridelike tone. "For a musician he has a most annoyingly precise mind."

"Scientist's mind too, you know."

"Is he really good as a physician? He seems totally disinterested in that now."

"He's really good," Gregory said. "Brilliant. And we need brilliance in that field. We're only at the primer stage in our knowledge of the glands."

"And when we're postgraduates, how dull! No disease, no amusing human aberrations, no war, no criminals!" She stretched luxuriously and threw him a malicious smile. "Allah il allah, there is no God but Glands. No human ill that can't be remedied by proper nutrition, hormones and capsules. What happens to religion in that set-up, Gregory? I listened to your delightfully modest homily the other evening and was properly impressed— after a fashion. But confess now, if the gland theory is carried to its logical conclusion, then your God is just a celestial pharmacist who has practiced his trade with criminal stupidity some thousands and tens of thousands of years."

"You're arguing from—"

"And if the human race in its comparatively short time on this planet manages to conquer the secret of gland behavior, then we are the real Gods, and your Unknown is simply an office boy who bungled the prescriptions until we dismissed him. In other words—no god."

"There's always an unknown equation," Gregory said. "You know very well I wasn't discussing an anthropomorphic God the other night, I was discussing that unknown equation. Every doctor comes up against it at some time or another. All of us come up against it. How does it happen that one individual conquers the handicaps of poor environment, hereditary defects, glandular abnormalities, to become what we call a good citizen, while another, with apparently everything in his favor, is a headache?" he ended ingloriously.

Iris toyed with a cigarette, laid it back on the table. She smoked seldom and when she did, voraciously. The cigarette was a temptation; she enjoyed tossing it aside. So few people knew the true secret of hedonism: to deny oneself ninety-nine small things, deliberately; to grant oneself the hundredth temptation not only deliberately but with wide-open, unrepentant eyes. Her thumbnail slashed the cigarette so that tobacco spilled from its sides.

Gregory said, "Queer, isn't it? I still remember the war shortage and feel chagrined when I see a cigarette wasted."

She lifted mildly surprised eyebrows. "But I didn't want it."

"And now no one else will."

She laughed. "That's right. I'm extravagant and possessive." She stood up and turned the full warmth of her enchanting smile on him. "But I can also be meek and generous. Come on. I'll sing a little for you if you'd like, since Tay isn't here."

Gregory followed her into the house and felt the need of saying defensively, "But he's tremendously enthusiastic about your voice, Iris."

"I know, he's at me to practice all the time." He helped her adjust the piano lid. "But I don't feel any real pleasure in singing for him. He's too intense, he doesn't relax. He's listening to something else, something behind the song."

"He's a musician himself, poor chap, he's analyzing," Greg pointed out. "I can guess how it is. I took a snap course once in musical appreciation and lived to regret it. I'd go to a symphony and be so busy identifying woodwinds and all the rest, so conscientious about knowing the when and wherefore of each movement that I couldn't see the wood for the trees! I've forgotten most of it now fortunately. These days I'm one of the great unwashed who just sits back and enjoys it."

"Bless you, my child. I wish there were more of you in every audience." Iris added casually, "Not that I ever had a professional audience. I've never sung in public." She riffled through the music. "Any pets?"

"How about *Il est doux, it est bon?*"

"That's a climax, not a beginning," she rebuked. "Let me limber up with simple things. Are you going to accompany?"

"Sorry. I can pick out things with one finger and that's all." He seized a slim green book from the cabinet and thrust it in front of her as she sat down to the piano. "If you're looking for something simple . . . here, I'll wager you don't know any of our college songs. Every American youngster is brought up on *Juanita* and *Seeing Nellie Home* and all the rest. No matter how it pains you, you must learn them all."

"All?"

"Yes," Greg said solemnly, "or small children will follow you on the street and point the finger of derision."

Her eye ran down the list of contents. "I think I know *Just a Song at Twilight*," she said doubtfully.

"No others? Not even *My Bonnie Lies Over the Ocean?*" He clasped his hands in mock entreaty. "But surely you know *Home, Sweet Home?* Why, you couldn't have managed an American visa without that!"

Iris sat very still and her smile only touched her lips. "I can sing *My Bonnie* and *Home, Sweet Home*," she said finally.

"Good." Gregory sat down to one side of the piano, where he could still watch her face. Iris played a chord or two, then sang *My Bonnie*. Her tones were tentative, soft at first, but she ended the song with assurance and Greg applauded, his face alight.

"Now *Home, Sweet Home*," he commanded.

"It's so saccharine."

"That's downright treason. If the greatest opera stars can sing it, why not you?" There was a teasing laugh in his voice. "Of course it's not easy to give freshness to anything so well-known. Perhaps it *takes* an opera star!" Iris still looked irritated. But suddenly her mood shifted and she slid him a slow, almost triumphant smile. "Oh, I can sing it," she assured him. "In fact when I'm through you

shall tell me who you have heard sing it better. But I
learned it without the piano score, without any score. I
shall sing it so."

She stood up and began: " 'Mid pleasures and palaces—"
her voice finding the key, the pitch, as unerringly as a
bird alights on a favored bough. Gregory sat very still,
feeling his heart pound with delight. The very absence of
any piano background gave her voice a nostalgic urgency,
as someone who sings lost and alone in a wilderness . . .
For Gregory the song was created. It was born for the first
time in this room. There was one small inaccuracy of
phrasing, he noted, almost subconsciously. She repeated
it, so it wasn't mere carelessness on her part. Whoever
had taught her the song had erred there, but the altered
phrasing was not unpleasant; somehow it made the song
more truly hers.

When she had finished he stood up and seized one of
her hands. It was cold and moist in his and she looked
unsmilingly at him, her eyes shadowed. "It was wonderful, Iris. I've never heard it sung better. Nor as well."
He folded up the song book with a little motion of finality
and placed it back in the cabinet, far back. He hoped she
would never discover that trivial inaccuracy of hers. It
would trouble her as a musician and she would conscien-
tiously learn the song all over again, using the piano score.
And something unique might be lost irretrievably, the
song of Iris.

He went on briskly, "Now the *Herodiade*." But while
his ear applauded the unforgettable aria and the exquisite
technique that functioned so effortlessly, his heart was
still engaged with the earlier melody. Something about

the way she had sung *Home, Sweet Home* had seemed to
be for him alone. It wouldn't be robbing anyone to keep
it for himself. He would never ask her to sing it for a
larger audience.

They sauntered out to the terrace again a little later
and now Iris picked up a cigarette and accepted a light
from Gregory. "I reward myself," she smiled and pushed
the wall button. "Cocktails or tea?"

"Cocktails," Karen said sepulchrally as she appeared in
the doorway. "I hope I startled you. Don't get up, darling," to Greg. She flung herself into a chair, long legs
outstretched, and pushed her soft felt to a comical cone on
the back of her head. "Goodness, I wouldn't believe it
could be so warm for this time of year. The train was
sizzling."

"Tay was coming out on the 5:10 too," Iris said.

"He must have taken the 4:40. He was in the garden
just now when I cut across lots. He's stopped to talk to
the gardener—if you can call that ancient mariner of yours
a gardener. I don't believe he knows a rhododendron
from an hydrangea and cares less. In fact," Karen added
doubtfully, "I just took the liberty of suggesting to Rafferty that he shouldn't uproot a perfectly good plant. He
was inclined to take a poor view of my advice but with
Tay's support I won."

"Thank you," Iris said graciously. "I know nothing of
flowers. You must advise me as well as Rafferty."

"My fee is a Manhattan. And what have you two been
doing?"

"Trying to get a word in edgewise," Gregory said
equably. "Iris has been singing for me."

"Oh, I'm sorry I missed it! I haven't heard you yet, Iris."

"You'll have enough of it eventually. Soon you'll be dodging me. And you'd better not enthuse to my husband because I've refused to sing for him the last two or three days. He might be—hurt." She turned as Ester appeared. "Manhattans and some Scotch, please. And tea for Dr. Harrison," she added as Taynor came up from the lawn and seated himself on the top step, his back against a stone pillar of the balustrade.

"Still virtuous, Tay?" Gregory asked admiringly.

"Still virtuous," Tay drawled. He grinned up at his wife from where he sat at her feet. "My strength is as the strength of ten because my heart is pure. Righto, Guinevere?"

Iris grimaced. "I don't believe it's virtue, but some mysterious ailment you're cherishing. Not that I want to hear about it, even if you two doctors want to talk shop."

"Greg's only a doctor in the bud," Karen declared, "and consequently twice as gory as the finished article. It takes constant vigilance to keep our dinner conversation edible." She spoke from the surface of her mind for her eyes were on Tay's lean brown hand where it rested on the floor. Iris' small slipper was only an inch or two away. It would be natural, almost inevitable for his hand to stir that fractional distance and rest on the slipper, a casual enough caress for a bridegroom even in public. But of course, Karen thought hastily, Iris was really a Continental, and Continentals were always horrified at the easygoing way with which Americans aired their emotions. She looked away and found her brother's eyes fixed on hers. A slow flush rose in her cheeks.

"Only two more days and we're off to Canada," she began volubly. "Day after tomorrow, in fact. You'll simply have to take your mackinaw, Greg. That suede jacket of yours is repulsive. And I think two pairs of your long woollies have shrunk."

"They were probably washed in boiling water," Greg moaned. "You should have laundered them yourself, a small enough thing for a doting sister to do."

"Why didn't you stand over the laundress?" Karen retorted unfeelingly. "Never mind, you'll be warm to your knees and elbows, at least." Ester appeared with the laden tray and Tay sprang up to help her. Karen fell abruptly silent now, as though the polite confusion around the table had relieved her of some necessity to chatter. Gregory studied his sister thoughtfully. What necessity? Karen wasn't naturally talkative for the sake of talk. She was capable of long comfortable silences, one of her loveliest qualities he had always thought. But recently he had noticed that she was running in high gear a good deal of the time, particularly when they were with the Harrisons. It was as though any momentary pause in the conversation threw her into a panic from which she rescued herself with chatter. Good thing her voice was low and on the husky side . . .

His hand paused in the act of lighting a cigarette. Now he remembered. He had caught her eyes fixed where his own had been fixed, on Tay's hand. Gregory thought: It mustn't be that way with Karen too. She's too candid, too easily hurt. She isn't even a would-be pirate. It's just that

she's hero-worshiped so long, she can't realize yet that
Tay is a married man, not to be tagged and nagged and
mothered any more. Perhaps she hasn't even guessed the
real nature of her feeling for him; perhaps she never will,
with any luck. When she knows the Harrisons better, sees
their mutual preoccupation, realizes the inviolability of
their relationship she'll straighten out. She simply needs
to see Tay once and for all as a married man, a bridegroom. When she does see him so—well, she has sense and
humor and pride.

He took the Scotch Tay handed him and said suddenly,
"Look here, why don't you two go along with us? Salmon
fishing, hunting, the big woods. You always loved it, Tay.
And it would be a whole new world even for a traveled
damsel like you, Iris."

"Iris isn't used to the cold," Karen said, looking down
into her glass. "She'd enjoy it more another year when
she's acclimated." Oh, the poor idiot, she was thinking
with despairing affection, does he want to crucify himself?
She had seen her brother's eyes on Tay's hand. Her casual
speculation had suddenly become an intuition of Greg's
tension. He had been afraid that Tay would touch Iris'
slipper—in front of his eyes.

"It would be marvelous having you with us," she went
on. "Dad would love it as much as Greg and I would, so
don't think I'm inhospitable. But it really can be cold,
particularly if we have a stretch of rainy days."

Tay said consideringly, "Yes, afraid you're right. Iris
is better off here. A bad cold, anything that might affect
her throat, her singing—"

Iris stirred in her chair, clasped her hands behind her

head. For some time she had been silent, busy with her
hostess duties. Now her eyes slid from Gregory to Karen,
then to her husband. "Well, I don't know, Tay. It might
be fun. I love new places."

"You wouldn't like the north woods," Tay said sharply.
"You're a jungle flower and there's no central heating. I
don't want you barking all winter, now that your voice is
just getting into shape again."

"It's my own voice."

"Is it? I think it might matter to a great many people.
And besides," he injected a teasing note into his argument, "hasn't a bridegroom any rights? Much as I enjoy
Littlefield Lodge, I'd rather like to have you all to myself
a little longer. Selfish but traditional."

From under the smooth white eyelids Iris shot a glance
at Gregory, who was just as studiously gazing over the
lawn. She had been right about him then. He had already reached the stage of rationing himself as far as
looking at her was concerned. She was glad he had that
much will power. The other type was too boring. "I think
we'll go," she said with lazy finality, "that is, if the Littlefields really want us."

Gregory looked at her now. "We do."

Karen made a last despairing attempt. "Of course we
do. But we don't want to be the death of you!"

"You won't be," Tay promised. "Iris stages everything,
even her own catastrophes. And speaking of catastrophes,
Iris, have you given thought to such little items as a whole
new rig for Canada? Boots, sweaters, heavy underwear—
a thousand things your silken little soul never dreamed of.
And less than two days to shop for them." He turned to

Gregory. "Your reservations are for the evening train day after tomorrow?"

Gregory nodded. Tay spread his hands. "There, you see? I doubt if we could get reservations this late."

"If not, then we could take a later one," Iris said calmly.

"Unless things have changed a lot since I've been there, it isn't a question of our taking a later train, or even of the Littlefields delaying their trip a day or two—even if we wanted to let them lose precious days of the fishing season. They can't wait anyway. It's a sixty-mile trip from Fredericton by car, then a two-and-a-half-hour truck jaunt from the highway into the woods. All those things have to be arranged well ahead. They're already arranged. The guides and the domestic help landed at the Lodge today. Right, Karen?" Karen nodded.

"There's no telephone to let them know of any change of plan. If we go at all, we'd have to go on that train day after tomorrow." Tay sat back. "I suggest we skip the idea."

Iris loathed hurry, loathed being rushed, loathed the pressure of time though she had felt it often. But it was obvious Tay didn't want to go and a small victory on that point would be agreeable. "If the right clothes are to be had, I can shop in a hurry," she said placidly. "Perhaps Karen would go with me as adviser. As for the train reservations, I never knew you to fail in that line."

"How about my affairs?" Tay asked in a professedly injured tone. "Is the lord and master supposed to drop everything on a moment's notice?"

Everyone laughed.

"That isn't your best excuse," Greg said, "not after you've loudly and often underlined the fact that your vacation is going on indefinitely."

Tay's shoulders moved in a little shrug of defeat. "Overruled, trampled on, snowed under! I only hope that Ester can locate my own camp duds somewhere in the attic. After all these years I haven't the faintest idea what trunks or boxes they're in."

"I have," Karen said promptly. "When they came from the warehouse I noticed how carefully your mother had marked everything of yours." Her breath caught a little and she looked away from Tay's suddenly darkened eyes. But for a second she had been alone with him, had traveled back with him to the quiet years that had seemed as permanent as they had proven evanescent. Tay's profile had turned away too, and she could glance at it again, the high aquiline nose, the brown hard cheeks, the tremendously broad shoulders, one of which jutted forward even now, as though he were perpetually ready to spring to his feet. Where, in what spot, through what circumstances, had he lost the strong tranquillity that had once been his salient characteristic? The strength was still there, but it was a strength that crouched. And the tranquillity had vanished, even if the lazy voice, the sure physical gestures were the same.

His glance moved from the garden, came back to the circle of the group. "Vacation or not, I shall have to get in some intensive business appointments. My lawyers have been yapping at me ever since I got back." He yawned. "May I have another slice of lemon, Mrs. Taynor Harrison?" And now as she took the cup his right hand moved,

hovered over the toe of Iris' slipper. It didn't settle however. He reached for a cigarette instead.

Gregory stood up. "Hadn't we better shuffle along,
Karen? You'll have to scramble to be ready for dinner as
it is. I'm delighted you two are going, Iris. And congratu-
lations on stirring Tay out of his lethargy. I think he's
simply afraid that he's lost his touch with a fishing rod."

Iris looked down, saw the look of secret amusement on
Tay's face. Though her smile didn't fade she felt a quick
thrust of anger, anger with herself. So. All along he had
wanted to go to Canada, intended to go. It was his little
victory, not hers. And it was too late now to reverse herself, without exhibiting a capriciousness that would leave
shrugging conclusions in the minds of the Littlefields.
Her good-bys were perfunctory, and with the departure of
her guests, her face darkened. She didn't trouble to
change for dinner that night and so, seated in the library,
she heard Tay's conversation over the telephone. Her
look was irritated as he hung up the receiver. "Why must
you stay at the Parker House tonight and tomorrow?" she
asked. "We're no distance from Boston."

He turned a politely patient face. "I told you there
would be a number of things to take care of if we left so
soon. And my morning appointments will be early. It's
easier to wake up right there in town than to get up at an
unearthly hour here."

"I have much shopping myself," she pouted.

"You're driving in with Karen, aren't you? But I'll
make double reservations if you like."

"Don't trouble. I am weary with hotels," she said with
that odd turn of idiom that occasionally characterized her

speech. "And don't forget you must look over your own camp things. I won't know what you need."

He frowned. "I'd forgotten that. Well, I'll try to taxi out for an hour or two tomorrow afternoon."

"Then you may as well stay here tomorrow night," she pressed.

"If I've cleaned up all my appointments." And with that she had to be satisfied. Dinner was a silent affair and the taxi had arrived for Tay almost before Ester had finished packing his bag. Iris' sulkiness cleared abruptly as she followed him to the door and held up her face for the kiss he would have to bestow, with Ester hovering discreetly down the hall. "Big business man," she mocked, "so suddenly too."

Tay slapped his coat pockets, making sure of his gloves. "Well, I have to make a new will for one thing. I've procrastinated over that too long."

Her hands released his lapels, slid away. "Don't cut me off with a shilling, Tay. I warn you, I'd sue." Her cheek was soft as a peach under the amber hall sconces and her smile was provocative.

He laughed. "Not with a shilling, I promise you."

Ester stood waiting patiently, the heavy boots in her hands. She was a spare, big-boned woman in her fifties, with broad flat cheekbones and a sallow complexion. Tay had been fortunate enough to secure her shortly after their arrival and consequently the domestic staff numbered four now, instead of three. Originally Ester was to have been upstairs maid and seamstress, with the understanding that she would assist Dana in the dining room when it was necessary. But Dana was old and crotchety, not too competent. Though nominally Dana still ruled the dining room and the downstairs, Ester was becoming more and more pervasive throughout the house.

Ester had a deft hand at mixing cocktails and Tay had gladly relinquished that privilege, as soon as Iris was satisfied that Ester was a teetotaler. Ester was a born ladies' maid, and though Iris didn't demand it, she didn't object when she found her bath water drawn, her underwear laid out; nor even when a thermos of hot milk had begun to appear unobtrusively on her bedside table at night. Just as unobtrusively the sleeping tablets had disappeared from that table and now reposed in the bathroom cabinet. Iris had smiled a little at that, but had said nothing. She wasn't too dependent on the pills anyway and eventually they would be bad for the complexion. And it was pleasant to have the kind of solicitous service that she hadn't known since the days in India.

What was more important, and unlike most competent people, Ester managed to get along with her less efficient colleagues. Dana had ceased to be possessive in her own sphere and Hulda, the cook, made no objection when Ester occasionally arranged an extra tray. Ester always left an immaculate kitchen and no important item ever disappeared from the refrigerators. Karen insisted that Ester had even wielded the lawn-mower on one occasion, but no one dared ask grumpy old Rafferty if that were true, so the matter remained apocryphal.

Iris, standing in front of the pier glass to judge the fit of her slacks and heavy jacket, glanced at the maid's reflection with satisfaction. No doubt some fly in the ointment would show up soon—it always did—but for the moment she could heartily approve of Ester. The jacket fitted perfectly and concealed the round line of her hips. "Have you any Korean blood, Ester?" she asked idly. "I hadn't thought of it before, but now—seeing you in the mirror—" She turned up a jacket cuff. Yes, they should be shortened a bit.

Ester said stiffly, "I hope I look thoroughly American, madam."

Iris swung around. "Oh, you do. It's just that mirrors have a little trick—" She smiled quickly, interrupted herself. "I've lived in the East most of my life and it's rather a habit of mine to speculate on racial stock. Much of the time I'm wrong. M'Dieu, those boots will be miles too big for me!"

"Not when you're wearing two or three pair of wool socks," Ester assured her. "If you'll sit down, Mrs. Harrison, we'll try them on."

"I wish you were going with us," Iris said a little fretfully, after Ester had been proved right once more.

Ester shook her head. "Everything's different up at the hunting lodge, madam. The help comes from the local towns, nice respectable people with their own little businesses, most of 'em. They don't think of themselves as domestics at all, just that they're doing you a favor. And in a way they are, to drop their regular work and run up to wait on you for three weeks."

"At a whopping wage, no doubt."

"People seem to think it's worth it." An austere smile edged her lips. "You needn't worry, Mrs. Harrison, they won't eat with you or be around you much, except the guides, of course. It's just that it's a lot more free and easy than it is here and you'll be happier if you sort of understand that, madam." She was trying the hip-length rubber boots on Iris now.

"They fit all right but they're terribly hot," Iris complained.

"After you've stood in a salmon river two hours you won't think so. It's like wading in ice." Iris was silent for a moment as Ester helped her strip off the boots and the heavy outer clothing. She stretched with relief, feeling her body free of everything but step-ins and brassiere. Suddenly she whirled around. "Have you been there, at Littlefield Lodge, Ester? You seem to know all about it."

"Not there, but I've worked for hunting people, madam," Ester said sedately. "I've heard 'em talk about it plenty. Now me, I wouldn't go for that sort of vacation. I like my easy chairs and warm radiators and good movies. But there, it seems as though the people who can afford

most anything like to be as uncomfortable as possible on
their vacations. Well, it takes all kinds to make a world.
Live and let live is what I say."

"Sometimes the two aren't compatible." Iris laughed
shortly.

"I beg your pardon, madam?"

"Nothing. Ester, I think I'm losing weight."

"That's what I've been thinking, Mrs. Harrison."

Iris said with some satisfaction, "Everything I have is
just a bit too loose. I wondered if the scales were wrong,
but if you think so too—"

"Definitely." Ester coughed and added carefully, "I
don't mean to presume but Dana says you're not hardly
touching your dinner these days. It doesn't do to diet too
strenuous. Such a pretty face, Mrs. Harrison, you don't
want to get it all lined."

Iris whirled to the mirror. There were no lines, no
slightest blemish, she saw with relief. But was there a faint
hardening of the outline, the merest suggestion that some
imperceptible bloom was retreating? Her mouth thinned
and she said harshly, "It's the rice, the damn rice! Every
night, every single night in the week!"

Ester looked puzzled. "But you never touch it, madam.
It's only Dr. Harrison who eats it."

"I have to *look* at it, don't I? The same dish every
night, until I could scream! No wonder I haven't an appetite for anything else either."

"It's a queer notion," Ester acknowledged, "though at
that I don't suppose it's any stranger than a person having
orange juice every morning like I do." And as you do,
madam, her tone implied delicately. "But I'm sure if

you were to speak to Dr. Harrison—" Her voice trailed.
She was not sure at all. She cleared her throat and went
on soothingly, "If I was you, I wouldn't look at the rice
at all, madam. And it wasn't on the table last night, was
it?"

"Because Dr. Harrison wasn't at home." Iris smoothed
the brief wisp of silk and lace that clung to her thighs. "I
think he will stay here tonight." She stared at her mirrored reflection critically, coolly. "That is, if he comes
back. But he said he'd have to, to look over his things. Are
they laid out?"

"On the third floor, the yellow bedroom. No sense clut-
tering up this room, madam."

"Well, let me know when he comes in, will you?"

"Yes, Mrs. Harrison." She moved silently about the
room, putting away the camp togs, as Iris sat down at the
dressing table and started creaming her face. Ester knew
when to talk and when to hold her peace. Presently she
picked up the jacket whose sleeves needed shortening and
left the room. She went directly to the combination linen
and sewing room on the third floor and opened the door.
Taynor was sitting on the window seat, smoking his pipe
in bland disregard for the lavendar-scented linens that rose
in serried ranks to the ceiling, shelf after shelf. He nodded toward a coat that was thrown across the sewing
machine in the corner.

"Two buttons off that, Ester. And see if you can mend
that pocket with the rubber lining, will you?"

Ester nodded and, tossing aside Iris' jacket, she crossed
the room and sat down by Tay. She pushed the mouse-
colored hair back from her forehead, sighed a little and

pulled a crumpled pack of cigarettes from some mysterious
pocket. "Tired?" Tay asked sympathetically as he struck
a match for her.

"There's plenty to do but I don't mind. I'm one that
has to keep on the go all the time or I get fidgety." She
took a puff of the cigarette, coughed genteely and said,
"The door panel is jammed. It isn't exactly open but it
won't shut clear. Sticks a bit. I fooled with it today every
chance I had, but I haven't any real business in that room
and Dana knows it."

Tay said, "I know it's jammed, that's what I came up to
tell you. I tried to get in just now but gave up. Afraid
I'd mess up some mechanism. We could probably fix it
ourselves if there weren't any interruptions. But we
couldn't be sure of that." He took a slip of paper and
handed it to her. "Toni's new number. I tried to get him
but he won't be back until tomorrow. Tell him he'll simply have to drop everything and get the door fixed. You're
not going until Thursday, are you? So you'll be able to
catch him."

"What'll Dana think? That room's part of her work."

"Tell her the piano tuner is coming," Tay said calmly,
"and that he's temperamental and must be left strictly
alone. The room's nearly soundproof and Toni can try
out the keyboard occasionally, enough to convince her.
Anyway, Dana won't hang around. There aren't many
sounds as maddening as a piano being tuned."

"Anything new in the room to tell Toni about?" Ester
asked.

"No, nothing. She hasn't sung for a week. Let Toni
look them over if he likes but you can tell him from me

that only the first two are any good from my point of
view. And probably no good from yours." His tone had
a small bitter edge, but she ignored that.

"Want him to take any back with him?"

He shrugged. "Let him do as he pleases." He emptied
his pipe, put it away and thrust his hands into his pockets.
"We don't seem to be progressing much, do we?"

"She wondered if I had Korean blood."

"What on earth—?" He burst out laughing. "And you
a born Vermonter, a descendant of Ethan Allen, with a
down-east accent that could be cut with a knife! She
wouldn't recognize that, of course."

Ester looked affronted. "I haven't *stayed* in Vermont all
my life," she said tartly, "not that I'm ashamed of my
accent. I like it."

"Of course you do, it's wonderful. *You*'re wonderful."
He patted her hand. His eyes were still pleased. "Indi-
cates something anyway, doesn't it? I mean it shows that
she's seeing Koreans or Chinese around every bush. Or
Filipinos. Not what you'd see if you had a good conscience."

Ester was unimpressed. "Frankly, it doesn't prove anything to me. Like she said, she's lived in the East and she's
used to guessing at racial mixtures."

Her tone was so decided that Tay's eagerness faded.
"Well, anything else?"

"The rice business is getting her down."

"Are you sure?"

"She's losing weight on it. But," Ester warned him,
"that doesn't prove anything either. It would get any
woman's goat to see a man tucking away rice every night

of his life. She could be innocent as a dove and it would still get on her nerves." She shot him a direct look over her cigarette. "And I can't say I like it myself, Tay. It smacks more of sadism than justice to me."

Tay said roughly, "Perhaps I know more about the justice of this case than you do."

"You *think* you do," she pointed out. "You're trying to prove it and I'm here to help you if I can. But the fact is you *haven't* proved it yet and until you do, this rice business isn't right. It isn't professional. Now with the music, that's different. That's scientific, Toni says. And anyway it's something that can't hurt nor harm however things turn out."

She ground out her cigarette in the tray. "So there's no luck on that."

"No," he said moodily and stood up to pace about the room. "There's plenty of proof to me but not what you people are looking for. My God," he burst out, "what more do you want than what you already know yourselves —and what I've told you!"

"Has to be an absolute identification," Ester said evenly, "beyond the shadow of any reasonable doubt. Our hands are tied until we get that."

"Well, my hands aren't tied indefinitely!"

Ester's face was pale. "I've thought of that lately," she said, "I've thought of it, but somehow or other I haven't passed the idea along. Maybe I should. Maybe it's my duty to."

Tay said mockingly, "Why? They won't do anything about it, not while there's a shadow of any reasonable doubt."

"I'm not just thinking of what *you* might do," she said evenly. "Ever occur to you that if you're right about her —well, maybe you're not in such a soft spot yourself?"

"It doesn't worry me."

"You're counting on her essential stupidity. But a woman like that doesn't need brains, Tay, she has something better. She thinks with her antennae. And if her feelers ever wave around and touch on what you're really thinking—curtains for you."

Tay said hardily, "I think her antennae have already touched on it. But she's not quite sure yet."

"Tay, how *could* she have guessed? No, you're wrong. She'd never have married you!"

"Oh, I didn't drop any clues until we were safely here in America, here at the house."

Her eyes widened in disbelief. "You don't mean you've deliberately tipped her off?"

"Not in so many words. But a spoor here and a scent there, if she cares to put them together."

"You had no right—" she began sternly.

He was unperturbed. "I never did care to take a pot-shot at a sitting duck. Particularly when the sitting duck is my wife."

"Let me remind you this isn't a game."

"It is to me." His voice was very hard. "The first real game I've had in two years. I've given her an even start, better than an even start. Now devil take the hindmost."

"So you think it's a game about to end." Ester's face was expressionless. "Well, I'll tell you, it's a game that's just begun. You're not the only one that makes the rules, you know. She makes them too."

"Not here, not now, not with me."

"Yeah?" she drawled. Then her face quickened as she watched him clench and unclench his hands. "Listen, Tay. Are you the only one who's suffered in this business? No. You're just one of several dozen, maybe hundreds. It isn't your private duty or responsibility. Not even your marriage makes it so, just the contrary."

"Whose duty is it, then?" he asked savagely. "No one gave a damn until I started putting dynamite under a bunch of doddering Colonel Blimps!"

The friendliness faded from Ester's face. Of a sudden it was very still and cold. When she spoke her voice was free of its Vermont drawl, it was crisp and sharp. "Perhaps it's about time to tell you that if you'd kept out of this entirely, the matter might have been wound up by now, one way or the other. Unless we could prove the identity—and we had even less to go on then, remember—there was no way of holding her except by stalling on the visa. We were doing that nicely and we might have gotten somewhere. That is, if you hadn't married her almost overnight and thrown a monkey wrench into the machinery." Her voice was trenchant. "By the time we got wise and contacted the consulate it was too late. It was done. Now you're no good even as a witness, since you're her husband, not a court witness anyway. The defense would blast you to smithereens. Get it, wise guy?"

Tay looked startled and she went on relentlessly, "What's more, it may interest you to know that you were under suspicion yourself after that very sudden marriage. We started checking and double-checking you from the very moment of the ambush, right through every day in

the prison camp and every step you took on your way to
Lisbon. And then we went back to your very beginnings.
By the time you sailed," she added coolly, "we could have
told you your grammar school record and the year you
wore braces on your very excellent teeth. Nineteen twenty-
three, as I remember."

Tay's eyes were startled. *"I* was under suspicion?"

"Why not?" she snapped at him. "Oh, you're in the
clear now. I simply mention it to show that there're always two sides to this sort of business, to any business
where identification means—death." She sat back, relaxed,
and her voice was pleasant again. "Don't look so stunned.
I told you, you're in the clear now."

"I never thought of the witness stuff," he muttered,
"when I married, I mean."

"I know." She was quiet. "You were only thinking that
she might slip away again if you hadn't some excellent
way of keeping her under your thumb. It was very tena-
cious of you, very sacrificial." Her tone was dry. As he
looked away she relented, went on more gently, "Oh, I
know. You were thinking of sad homesick words in the
night and a cry for help. And you were thinking of the
sequel to that cry, of men rotting in the muck. And more
than that—of men watching their own skeletons grow."

Tay said, dully, vaguely, "The men, yes. But that's war
perhaps, of a sort. There were other things, worse things
. . . A missionary family, for instance, so well hidden by
the Moros that they couldn't have been safer in a Boston
hotel."

"Yes?"

"They listened too, the parents and the three children.

They listened while she sang for them." His smile was quite dreadful. "I saw the little girl later, just out of the corner of my eye. She couldn't have been more than five years old and her hair was still in neat little yellow pigtails. It hadn't been mussed at all. Not at all," he added thoughtfully.

Ester sprang up and struck her arm in a kind of passion across her thin chest. "My God, Tay, how can you sleep in that room!"

There was a long silence, then he said with an effort at jauntiness, "I was at the Parker House last night. But I see I have one convert at least. You know what she is."

Ester looked down at her broad square hands. She had always adjudged herself as unimaginative, but she had a trenchant inner eye that occasionally disconcerted her. So now the picture rose before her though she couldn't have put it in words: the pond lily swaying on its hollow stalk, its ivory and gold loveliness apparently drifting with the water's whim; but still anchored to its real kinship, the native slime. She watched, fascinated, the small crawling things march back and forth, back and forth from the coarse yellow heart to the ineffable smoothness of each petal edge. And the lily's heavy sweetness was unperturbed, untouched. Most lovely, most foul lily. Most inevitable lily, for the slime too must labor and bring forth according to its nature, according to the nature of some unknown equation.

"I don't know," she said at length. "Maybe I believe with my heart if not with my mind. Or maybe it's just your belief that's hypnotized me. It's hard to think sanely in a house full of hate, Tay. Much as I like you, when I

see you with her it's like being alone with two dreadful
strangers. Not one, but two. It's like being in a stinking
fog along a Canton waterfront. You can't see the junks
but you can smell 'em. You hear a laugh, a snatch of gib-
berish that wouldn't make sense even to a Cantonese
porter. You hear the creak of a pole pushing against something that isn't there. And a wailing perhaps. And you
don't know whether it's one of those screechy lullabies—
or a man overboard. I tell you, you can be part of it without even knowing what it's all about. And I was a part
of it."

"Was Iris right? Do you have Oriental blood?" Tay
looked at her curiously.

"Not Korean. My maternal great-grandfather was Ha-
waiian-Japanese," she said bluntly. "I had a wandering
foot myself and spent more than half my life traipsing
around the East, anywhere I could get a job—and I could
always get one. Listen, I know most of Japan and part of
the China coast like I know the back of my hand, much
better than I know Vermont." She flung that hand out
defiantly. "*Now* how do you feel about me, big boy?"

"No differently." His smile was exhausted but un-
changed. "I like and admire you a great deal, Ester."

She stared at him and flushed and her voice was wistful.
"Do you really like me, Tay?"

"Yes."

She moved toward him and laid large, spatulate hands
on his shoulders. Her plain sallow face lifted to his with
a sort of stern tenderness. "Then I'm going to say something. I'm not an endrocrinologist—is that the word?—but
there's not much I don't know about people and life,

Tay. I've seen and heard about everything and I don't shock easy. But there's an ugliness in this house that I don't like. Oh, I understand it but it still makes me sick, sick to my stomach. You know what it is."

His shoulders were rigid under her hands but she went on steadily. "It's an ugliness in the night, an ugliness that could wreck you, Tay, without ever touching her."

He stared at her unbelievingly. "You accuse me of— cruelty?" His face flamed.

"No," she said, "no. Nothing as simple." Her eyes were very quizzical and kind and now her hands dropped from his shoulders and went akimbo to her hips. "You know, sometimes it's pretty convenient to pretend to ourselves that we're warped, to pretend that we're so snarled up with pain and horror that we're hardly responsible for what we do. That way we can indulge ourselves, can't we? That way we can get away with murder and still kid ourselves."

She crossed the room and sat down at the sewing machine, dismissing him. "Not," she added mildly, "but what to my mind there aren't a lot of things worse than a good clean murder . . . By the way, Mrs. Harrison wanted to know when you came in. You'd better speak to her now. Shall I tell Hulda you'll be here for dinner . . . and breakfast?"

"I shall not be," Tay said savagely. "I have an appoint- ment in town tonight. You can pack all the things on the bed in the yellow room. I'll be back tomorrow in time to take Mrs. Harrison to the station." He stalked out of the door and closed it behind him with polite restraint, but his face had still been very red indeed under its tan.

Ester reached for thread and needle. "Anyway, thanks

for the use of the hall, Dr. Harrison," she said aloud. She smiled to herself and picked up his coat. It had been suavely cut but it had seen hard usage. It would stand quite a bit more wear too, for though the material had a surface roughness, it was closely knit and durable. She looked at it with contented approval. A few rather important stitches and it would be as good as new.

6

THE NEXT morning, her packing completed, Iris went to the kitchen for a last admonishing talk with Hulda. Halfway down the stairs she paused. The hall mirror reflected a corner of the music room and her eye noted that the familiar reflection was distorted, so that the music room gave the absurd illusion that its wall was caving inward. But Hulda was waiting and Iris' eye rather than her mind had been troubled. The mirror must be askew. Concluding her instructions to the cook, Iris turned to Dana. "And the hall mirror needs straightening. Take care of it, will you?"

"It's high and hangs very heavy, ma'am," Dana objected. "I'm not so good on a stepladder with my rheumatism and bad legs. Maybe if Hulda was to help me—"

"Ester and Hulda help you quite too much as it is," Iris said crisply. "You'll take care of it yourself." She glanced down at Dana's swollen and misshapen ankles and her voice took on a thin edge of distaste. "That's an order, legs or no legs." But that evening when she went to the car she noted that the music room wall still seemed distorted in the mirrored image.

"Dana will have to go," she said to Tay as he placed the rug over her knees and the car started away. "She does less every day."

"No ball of fire," Tay admitted comfortably, "but the poor old bird shouldn't be working at all with those game legs of hers. Give her credit for trying to keep off the welfare lists."

"Are you a private charitable organization?"

"No," he admitted again, "I can't afford the luxury and Ester does most of Dana's work, I know. But it won't kill us to give Dana these two or three weeks of rest before she has to tackle an unkind world again. Matter of fact, she was showing anxious signs of life when I came back this afternoon. There she was perched on a ladder trying to straighten the hall mirror."

"I told her to straighten it, but she didn't."

"No. I made her come off the ladder in a hurry. No sort of job for a wobbly old woman. And she must be half-blind too. The mirror wasn't crooked."

"*I'm* not half-blind," Iris said sharply. "Either the mirror is crooked or one of the walls of the music room is coming apart. And I don't suppose you will claim that's the case, even to defend Dana."

Tay lit a cigarette. "My error," he said, when the cigarette was finally drawing, "so the mirror is crooked . . . Marvelous evening, isn't it? But it'll be cold later when we get near the border, and along in the early morning the train is drafty as the dickens. You'd better turn in with woollies instead of chiffon."

But Iris was silent. Her mind now, and not her eye, was on the mirror. Her physical vision had always been quick to note even the minute details of her surroundings —it had had to be—and now she did not doubt her photographic memory. Tay had implied that she had been wrong, that she had deliberately set Dana an awkward and unnecessary task. Iris would not have minded that.

Even an unnecessary task would serve Dana right. But Iris did mind Tay's rebuke. It was more important than ever that he stop accumulating these tiny little items to her discredit. He seldom commented but it was tiresome to be always on guard. It was becoming more and more restful to be with Gregory, Gregory who saw everything she did from another angle, in the light of his infatuation.

Another angle . . . her mind returned nigglingly to the mirror. It must still be crooked for the music room wall couldn't be out of plumb. She visualized the room, bounded by the side hall, the terrace and the living room on three sides; by the corridor to the terrace on the fourth; or rather, by the big coat closet off the corridor. But Tay was speaking now and she had to answer him. Presently they were walking to the gates in the North Station where the Littlefields were waiting. There was a glitter about all three of them, Iris thought half-sullenly, as though they had come even more alive in the premonitory cold of the station. The commuting hour was long over and around them at the same gate were similar groups, some of them laden with gun cases or rods; but all of them wearing that same expectant sparkle. What were they excited about? To be going from their bleak cold New England to an even bleaker, colder Canada? Or perhaps this odd species only felt real warmth when it was misted with frost.

Iris shivered and stared at Karen after the lively greetings had been exchanged. Karen's face under the saucy brown felt with its red hunter's feather had for this moment, at least, an authentic beauty. Her coloring, even the odd triangle of her face seemed inevitable. When she turned her face laughingly up to Tay, the lights caught diamonds from underneath the thick black lashes. Iris answered Gregory's inquiries smoothly enough, but her eyes slid from Karen to Tay.

For the first time she saw him spontaneously aware of a woman as a woman. Oh, he had been aware enough of her, Iris. But it had never been spontaneous. It had always been an awareness that she had had to scheme for, to work toward, to ambush, as it were; and that very fact had allowed Iris to feel comfortably assured in one field of rivalry at least. Now she felt uneasiness as the tentacles of her thought groped hesitantly toward those two.

Judge Littlefield said at her elbow, "It's Karen's type of costume, isn't it?"

Iris smiled. "Yes, I was just thinking that. Your young American girls are so delightfully angular, all coltish limbs and collarbones. They're decidedly at their best in sports clothes."

His eyes twinkled down at her. "Coltish limbs, perhaps. But I'll have to defend my daughter's collarbones. You've never seen her in evening dress, have you? Her apparent slimness is quite deceptive. However," he added thoughtfully, "I'll have to admit she's not exactly the boudoir type."

"Do you classify everyone, even your own daughter?"

"A habit from years on the bench," he conceded.

"And what is the boudoir type?"

His amused smile deepened. "I recommend the movies to you, Mrs. Harrison. And now if you'll excuse me I'd better check with our porters."

Iris' look followed him as he strode away. He was a

young looking fifty-five, especially in that casual attire. His shoulders were broad under the heavy jacket and his gray hair was as thick and crisply curling as Gregory's. For the first time she considered him as potential conquest and her inner look was thoughtful. Underneath that pleasantly sardonic manner of his did he wear as defenceless an idealism as characterized his son? She doubted it and the doubt stirred an agreeable excitement. Judge Littlefield was big game. Too big game, she decided reluctantly, and put the excitement behind her. She had her hands sufficiently full with Taynor, and Gregory would be a safe enough amusement on the side. Better to keep Judge Littlefield in the niche he occupied now, a platonic onlooker who found her amusing, shallow and obvious.

Iris did not mind people finding her obvious. That very obviousness was in itself a protective coloring, especially from the more shrewd minded. But now she glanced around. Gregory too had left her. She was standing alone and a few feet away Taynor was still animatedly teasing Karen about her hunting prowess.

"If I don't get a deer, I'll copy a score for you," Karen was boasting.

"I'll take the feather in your hat instead," Tay said. "It must be that, that makes you look so perky tonight."

"Perky! That's a heck of a compliment."

"If I started on authentic ones I wouldn't know when to stop."

Karen flushed and throwing out a hand caught at Iris' arm. "He's teasing me," she appealed. "He gave me my first shooting lesson years ago and he still can't believe that I've learned to hit anything smaller than a barn door."

Iris' smile was warm, denting one smooth cheek with just the suggestion of a dimple. "I sympathize. Tay has an airtight mind. It takes him forever to revise a judgment." Under the smile her vague discontent crystallized for the first time into an active dislike of Karen.

She slept poorly that night. In spite of the blanket some chill that wasn't physical seemed to have settled around her. From the depth of sleep she sat up abruptly and switched on the berth light. Karen, she thought bewilderedly, am I worrying about Karen? No, it wasn't Karen, it was a wall. Almost without volition she reached for her handbag, drew out a pencil and a slip of paper. In a few swift strokes she had drawn a crude diagram. Here was the deep coat closet, about seven feet long and perhaps five feet wide. But the music room was at least seventeen feet long; so was the corridor. And on neither side of the partition was there any jog or setback.

Then where had a space approximately ten by five vanished to?

She thought: A space too big for a disused chimney shaft, but enough for a small room. There must have been a door once, but where had it been? The corridor was papered. But the music room was paneled. Easy enough to conceal a door in paneling. Easy enough too for a careless person to leave the door ajar so that glancing in a mirror . . .

She shuddered down into the blanket again but her forehead was damp. She fought against this unreasoning panic as long years ago she had fought and resolutely stifled all the agonized night-thoughts, the weak and sleazy ghosts of her convent years. Suppose there were a room, originally planned for some prosaic enough purpose and later found unnecessary? What of it? Surely she would have thought nothing of it if that same empty space had been in juxtaposition to any other portion of the house. It was simply that the music room held her secret dread. Ridiculous to be afraid of a room, a walled-up, disused room. Yet there it was, she was afraid. She crumpled up the paper and thrusting it back into her handbag, settled into her pillows resignedly and lit a cigarette. There was only one thing to do with the fear: go back through the years and find the room that had originally planted this seed of panic in her mind.

The room in Montmartre into which her father had stalked, just as she and Jules had settled down to the cheap red wine and the omelet? She could see that room plainly enough, the tumbled red plush couch, the coarse lace curtains stiff with soot, the candles with tipsy pink shades over their guttering eyes. A smile edged her lips. The Frenchman had been frightened enough but Iris had been relieved. Her brief infatuation had not even run the length of her eighteen hours of married life. She had listened demurely as her father threatened and her husband pleaded. In the end, she had walked through the door without even a backward glance for a middle-aged man who, with head buried in his arms, was crying ludicrously at the table. Ludicrous, because a lock of his black hair was touching the omelet that he had cooked with such wizardry over a gas jet such a short time before.

Outside in the mean street her father had turned to her.

"He really thought you were twenty," he muttered, excusing himself for not having taken harsher measures against the man. And then, since they were in Montmartre, he had taken her for a real dinner in a little café he knew. For the first time he had let her have champagne, in tacit recognition of her status as a married woman, even though she was only sixteen. Eventually they had both laughed uproariously over the gas-jet omelet and the black pompadour enmeshed in its melancholy, deflated surface.

No, Iris thought contentedly, it wasn't that room. That room had actually spelled the beginning of her real companionship with her father. Her thoughts moved on.

The room in India where her father had lain dying? No, because she hadn't felt panic then. She had only felt very sorry that she had had to leave him. He had been rather unreasonable toward the end of their argument and she had been almost glad of that, for it had made her impatient, stiffened her in her resolve. "But, my God, 'Ris, you *can't* leave me!" he had whispered. "It'll only be a few days, perhaps even a few hours. You can wait that long. The servants have all skipped except Ghafur, and he'll go if you do. 'Ris, stay with me!"

But, of course, she had had to go. Neither the train nor the cooling ardor of a certain male would wait for her father to die. "You'll be all right," she had said soothingly. "You're improving every day, that's why you're feeling so bad-tempered. By the time I'm back you'll be sitting up again." He had closed his eyes then in tired denial and murmured, "At least give Ghafur his back wages, and enough more so he'll stay on with me."

"I will," Iris had promised. And she had meant it too,

until she had discovered that her best luggage had mil-
dewed and that she'd have to buy expensive new bags in a
hurry, without even time for the usual haggling. In the
end her father had wept also, just like the Frenchman.
But in this case Iris had looked back. Her own eyes had
been moist, she remembered, in a swift tenderness for that
pretty young thing who had had to leave forever the one
man who had ever really cared for her . . . Iris killed the
cigarette and wiped her eyes reminiscently. No, it hadn't
been that room. That room had meant urgency, for her
father had lingered too long over his dying; and it had
meant a grief that it had taken her days to rationalize and
a full fortnight to forget. But there was no panic in the
memory of the room.

The room where she had married Terry O'Hearn? No,
that ceremony had been held on a terrace.

But now Iris felt the nape of her neck tingle as her
thoughts scurried on, stumbling or leaping over a strange
and hazardous road that she had thought to put behind
her forever. The room in Yokohama, the small high room
in Yokohama . . .

She had stood by the piano, her knees shaking with
nervousness. And Fritz, turning over the leaves of the
music, had smiled encouragingly at her. "Make nothing
of it, the stage fright," he had said. "So it will make the
voice like a small girl's and that will be good. Think only
that you are one small cog in a great machine and feel
pride." Baron von Bohlen had been a rock of strength;
his eyes had been like sharp gray chips from that rock too.

There were only two others in the room, two small sallow men in correct "mornings" who sat whispering sibi-

lently to each other. "But it is so different, having no audience," Iris had stammered. Von Bohlen had nodded then toward the control room, where behind the plate glass one man sat before a switchboard and another bent over the recording machine; a queer room, embedded in silence as far away as the moon's. "There's your audience," Fritz had smiled. "The Pacific, half of Asia. And one day Asia will be the world." Then, as the second hand on the big clock kept jerking onward with stiff marionette steps, he had seated himself at the piano and added a final instruction. "You will sign off with *Home, Sweet Home*—without the piano. That way there will be more of the nostalgia, nicht? And less confusing for you since you have learned without the score from your so excellent first husband. Will you need the key?"

Iris had shaken her head. Mike fright or no, she was sure of her absolute sense of pitch. She was also sure that it was the control room that was the source of her nervousness: its insulated silence, its huge sardonic glass eye. And she had turned her back on it, adjusting the microphone to her new position. Now only the clock faced her, mincing and jerking along, telling off the seconds that would bring her to that final goal, to power. A fierce and heady elation had filled her . . .

Tay spoke suddenly from the bunk above her and Iris' hand gripped the sheet in a convulsive start. She had been so far away from this drafty swaying train that his voice struck her like a physical blow. "What's the matter? Are you ill or cold?"

She swallowed and said carefully, "I think I am developing a sore throat." Without protest she watched him descend the ladder and she submitted meekly as he took her temperature and peered down her throat. She was meek because she was filled with an infinite relaxation. She had tracked her unreasoning panic to its source and discovered only an ancient bogy man. The parallel was simple, she nodded to herself. Her first stage fright had been associated not only with a microphone and a piano, but with that silent walled-off room beyond, the control room. Natural then, that the first hint of an unknown room beyond the music room at home had produced the same panic.

She stretched luxuriously. That narrow rectangular space abutted the terrace. Originally, no doubt, it had been a flower room, walled off when the old conservatories had been torn down. That purblind old fool, Dana, had probably dislodged some catch on the paneling that had once been a door. But it was equally obvious that neither Dana nor anyone else had noted that telltale, jutting inch. Something amusing might be done with that space sometime, she wasn't sure what. A ghostly voice, perhaps, frightening Dana out of her last remnants of wits? Useful, if Tay proved stubborn about dismissing the woman. Still, that would be rather like employing an atom bomb on an ant hill! Gregory now, Gregory with his high-flown ethics and his half-baked smear of religion, Gregory with that mysticism so at physical odds with his stocky build and the light freckles on his blunt nose . . . Gregory was a natural for a hoax.

"You haven't a temperature and your throat looks all right," Tay was saying as he rinsed the thermometer. "You had me worried for a moment, thinking about your voice."

Her eyes dreamed up at him. "Sometimes I think my

voice is the only thing you care about as far as I'm concerned."

"Sometimes when I hear you sing, I think so too," he said cheerfully and replaced the thermometer in the case.

"Tay, I'd be much warmer if you slept with me. There's room."

"You'd better have my extra blanket. I don't need it." He pulled the sheet from her shoulders and surveyed their creamy roundness with an unkind and wholly professional eye. "I thought so. For the love of Mike, didn't you bring any flannels?" He pulled a sweater from a hanger and buttoned her into it against her outraged protests. Then he sat on the edge of the berth and took her wrist lightly in encircling fingers. "Listen, Iris, you were bound to go on this trip though I warned you might not like it. You'd better be prepared to be a grass widow for three weeks. Men and women bunk separately at the Lodge."

Iris frowned. "And you were away last night and the night before." Her voice rose to a fretful, sarcastic key. "You are most absurd, Tay. Are Lodge rules retroactive, clear back to the train we arrive on? Is it a law that my feet must be cold tonight and my throat sore because of some mythical deer that will no doubt escape me?"

"The deer is not mythical but it will no doubt escape you," Tay said. His hand went to the foot of the bed, reached under the covers. "And your toes are quite warm. The Lodge isn't the Ritz, Iris, nor yet Paris or Lisbon. A-hunting you must go. Diana is the role now. Put your mind to it and play the part as beautifully as you play every part—beginning now."

Ester and Toni were having a feast of reason and a flow of soul. They hadn't seen each other since the days in Burma when both had been not-too-humble cogs in the Strategic Services machine; and now Ester's drawl covered almost as much ground as Toni's more rapid Latin tongue. He paused for a moment in his spate of chatter, laid the last instrument down and triumphantly swung the paneled door back and forth. On the final motion it moved with a soundless grip back into the music room wall. There was nothing to indicate now that this was anything more than one of the many wall panels. "Try it," he said. Ester opened and shut it successfully.

"Let me open it from inside," she suggested, "I wouldn't crave to be shut up in there any length of time." She slipped into the inner room, closed the door. Toni waited. After a few seconds, he opened the door himself. "What's the matter?" Ester was vexed. "It still sticks from this side," she complained, "you'll have to do better."

Toni examined the catch, then the threshold and his voice was patient. "It's all right. Just lift up and move it easy, see? These soundproofed doors all have to sit tight as joints. It won't stick unless you yank and pull too hard."

"Well, all right," she grumbled. "Anyway, it's Tay has to bother with it, not me. Now you're in here, do you want any records? Not that it'll do you any good."

"She hasn't sung it yet? The sign-off? If she would only sing it once, just once, it would be her swan song," he added hopefully.

Ester shook her head. "Not her. She should be that dumb. Poor Tay." Toni closed the door and looked around the small space in which they stood. A concealed ventilator giving air from the terrace was the only connection with the outdoors; and a recording machine, a cabinet, two chairs and a wastebasket were the only furnishings. From the machine an arrangement of wiring led under the door, beneath the music room rug and so to various portions of the floor near the piano. Other wires, laid before the ceiling had been plastered, terminated in a chandelier directly above the Bechstein.

Ester selected a large disk from the cabinet. "Want to hear the first record?" she asked.

Toni's eyes gleamed. "Yeah," he said. "Boy, I haven't heard that voice for years." He took a cigarette from a crumpled pack but Ester shook her head.

"Not here," she said. She gestured eloquently at the metal basket which held the fine wax shavings plowed up each time the needle grooved a new disk. "That would make a nice little blaze with half a chance. And even with the ventilator it would take an age to air the room of smoke." Toni meekly replaced his cigarette as Ester inserted the disk and the record started playing. It came to a stop and she replaced it with another. Suddenly Toni's placidity broke, there was a brief white line about his mouth, as he listened. Yet the words he listened to were ordinary enough.

"You know—now that we're back in America and really

at home," Iris was saying, "we should celebrate. Let's shout *The Star-Spangled Banner!*"

The record revolved silently for an appreciable length of time before Tay's voice came in. "And I'm sure you could manage the high notes. But don't you think *Home, Sweet Home* would be more appropriate?" Again the record revolved silently. When Iris' voice came in again it was fainter, as though she were moving from the piano. "Enough singing for now. I'm sure it must be time for lunch. I'm hungry. I want my first meal in my first home."

Ester removed the record. "That's all," she said matter-of-factly, "and not much. But it's the best of any of them."

"When was the last record?"

"A week or more ago. Tay says she hasn't sung for days."

Toni drew a long breath and stood up. "The nerve of her," he said, struggling inadequately for words. "The nerve of her. *The Star-Spangled Banner!* I ask you. He almost got her at that. Look at the way she couldn't think what to do when he says sing *Home, Sweet Home.* Anyone listening to that would know she was struck dumb. I bet you could count twelve seconds slow, before she said a thing."

"You can't hang a body for not talking," Ester shrugged. "Maybe she was fixing her garter. Maybe she was wiping her nose," she added ironically.

Toni nodded. "Yeah. But that's the Voice all right. Me, I'd know it anywhere in a hundred years."

Ester's tone was edged with an even darker sarcasm. "Would you? I wonder. Voices aren't like fingerprints. Radios and records and phones do something to them. A lot of resemblances come out and a lot of differences are wiped out."

"Nobody in the whole wide world ever sang *Home, Sweet Home* the way Yokohama Lily sang it," Toni observed frowning, "with a whole wrong phrase in it. But sounding good, almost like an improvement—God help the composer."

"Someone else sang the phrase wrong too," Ester pointed out. "Jules Lefauvre, her first husband, the one who taught her."

"Dead now. And we checked his other pupils," Toni ruminated. "He never taught any of 'em that song. They were all French. But he thought it would make a hit with Iris because she was born American. And later when the Nips want her to pick something that'd make any G.I. homesick, she remembers it." His face darkened and that chilly storm swept across it again.

"She should've stuck to Yokohama and the radio station," he said softly. "That might've got her only a few years in the clink. She could've been just a laugh like Tokyo Rose, with everyone saying what the hell the war's over, where's my electric toaster or my new car and don't clutter me up with Tokyo Rose, that Ginza broad. But not Iris. No. She's got to have more dough. All the dough there is in Greater Asia, or all she could get."

Ester was thoughtful. "No, it isn't the money. At least, only as a means to an end. What she wants is plain power. Some people are downright sick without it; it's just like they're missing an arm or a leg."

She picked up the two mammoth disks and walked back into the music room. Toni switched off the light and fol-

lowed her, closing the paneled door. In a sort of tacit
consent they seated themselves on the window seat and lit
cigarettes. After a little silence, "What was the real story
on the Pacific business, Toni? My job was almost all here,
you know, checking Tay at this end."

"I don't know more than the outline myself," Toni said.
"It wasn't part of my job either. But as I get it, the Nips
hit on the idea of using her as a decoy for some of the resistance nests they couldn't get at. It only worked a short
time with the troops. Even so, a few hundred are rotting
in the jungle because of her. Then word got around and
she was shut off from the bigger outfits. But some of the
others . . . three families of missionaries, a bunch of an-
thropologists and a few other civilians I heard about—well,
they hadn't been able to get in touch with the world for
some time. Either they didn't have radios or the sets
weren't working any longer, so they hadn't been wised to
Yokohama Lily."

"Tay said something"—Ester's face was troubled—"but
you know how it is. When things are over you don't like
to ask questions. You want to put it all behind you and
get on with the next job."

"Yeah."

"But I'm worried about Tay. He hasn't gone at this
thing professionally, right from his marrying her. Yet
when you get to know him, you somehow feel he's sound
as a dollar underneath, tough but sound. That's why I'm
puzzled. Toni, if you do know some of the details, give.
After all, I'm here on this job and Taynor Harrison is almost as much a part of that job as Iris."

Toni said resignedly, "Look, if you want the psychology

stuff, go somewhere else. All I know is a few scattered facts and I'm not too sure of those."

"Anything. Maybe I could put it together and Tay would begin to make sense to me."

"Well, the resistance nests began getting under the Nip skins plenty. If they left 'em alone, as they did for a while, then the first thing they knew they had another organized guerrilla band on their hands. It was definitely not becoming funny. Even in the isolated sectors the Moros had too much nuisance value, playing ball with the enemy. So the Nips decided they'd have to draw up a definite campaign —take no more of this business. Iris was an ace in the hole. They shipped her here, there and everywhere, and she pulled in a lot of fish.

"First they tried her in the concentration camps, disguised as a prisoner, asking questions, trying to get a line on where the guerrillas or even the little isolated nests were holding out. But the prisoners didn't know much or they were too cagey. And some of 'em began to wonder about her, how she kept so plump and hearty while the rest of 'em were turning to skin and bone under her eyes. They say that's when she began to put on weight; made her hungrier, you know, seeing so many people starving."

Ester made a stifled sound in her throat but Toni didn't look at her. "Then a chap was brought in who thought he recognized her voice and she was almost lynched—until the Nips whisked her out."

"But she never talked on the radio. She only sang."

"She announced her own songs the first night she broadcast," Toni said, "but not after that. Maybe this prisoner heard her then. There's something about her voice any-

way," he said vaguely and went on. "So then the Nips took
her right into the jungles, using her as a straight decoy.
Small time stuff you might think, but it paid off for a
while. Some little gun nest that was blocking a trail or a
hill that it would cost too many men to rush, well, that
would be Iris' meat. She'd wander along a path, talking to
herself, singing a little song—like she had gone crazy with
suffering, see?"

"Another Ophelia," Ester murmured.

"Her, I wouldn't know," Toni admitted frankly. "But
if there were white men near by they'd come out to rescue
this poor soul and—pfft!"

Ester said admiringly, "I'll tell the world she took her
chances. Physical guts, at least."

"By that time she didn't have a choice," Toni pointed
out grimly. "She'd seen enough to choose an American
bullet rather than have her fingernails torn out by the
Nips—and a few other things."

"Yes," Ester said musingly.

"She got Tay that way."

Ester's astonishment was real. "In a gun nest? No. He
was medical corps."

"What do you think that was, a mahogany job? He had
dozens of medical units under him and that meant travel-
ing all over hell and gone most of the time. Oh, maybe it
was a combat outpost, if you want to be technical. Anyway, Tay was picked up with a batch of eighteen other
prisoners. There was a two-day march back to the Nip
camp. And even though he didn't see her close, he knew
there was a white woman with the Jap guards, the woman
with the voice he had heard."

Ester stood up and stared out the window. "I'm disappointed," she said. "Oh, I know Tay's patriotic, that he has a right to be ugly. But to be a one-man God of Vengeance?" She shrugged ruefully.

"For Chrissakes, don't you *want* her caught?"

"I'd like it better if Tay weren't doing it so—personally."

Toni stared at her, his face twisted into an honest grimace of concentration. "You women!" he said. "You women, I'll never get you. I suppose you could have seen the family, seen that little girl, and still want to draw Mrs. Harrison's bawth, madam, and then tuck her up in a nice clean jail with silk sheets and the latest magazines!"

Ester whirled on him and seized his arm so that he winced. "That's it! What family and what about it?" she demanded. "Tay said something so I got the general idea, but that was all."

Toni rubbed his arm and grumbled, "I'm out of training."

"Waiting," she said grimly, backed to the wall and folded her arms.

"Like I told you, there was a two-day march back to the Nip camp, and the Hiros thought they might as well make good use of the time. They knew that somewhere along the way there was a missionary family holed up with a batch of Moros. The father and mother were ill and the three kids were all under twelve, but the Nips wanted them and the Moros. So every night along the march Tay and the other prisoners had to hear this white woman doing her stuff, the stuff their sentries had fallen for. The mutterings and the calling for help and the little sentimental songs. They didn't hear much, of course, because

the woman was sent on ahead. But they did hear the
Home, Sweet Home. That was the pay-off. It was a hot
guess it was Yokohama Lily herself, though they could
hardly believe she's be out there in the jungle.

"But the missionary family didn't know and the Moros
didn't have enough English to explain it to them. The
Moros had good sense though. When they couldn't get
anywhere in their argument, they tied and gagged the parents and beat it to the brush with the kids—all but the
little girl who slipped away from them somehow. Poor
kid, even at five, even born in the jungle, she knew her
American songs, just like a parrot would."

"Oh, my God," Ester said.

"Yeah." Toni was dry. "Only He wasn't looking just
at that moment. When Tay saw her, the kid's head was
in one ditch and the rest of her in another."

"Her hair was in pigtails," Ester said in a tight voice,
"yellow pigtails. And they weren't mussed."

Toni stared at her. "If you know it all, what are you
putting me through it for?" His tone was sour.

"That's the one thing I heard. Go on."

"One of the Moros scouted around and saw a good bit
of what happened. Tay was the only doctor in the bunch
so the Nips tried to use him to keep the parents alive until they'd finished the—questioning. They wanted to get
the others in the family and especially the Moro bunch."

"Did they?"

Toni looked away. "No. They didn't get the little boys
or the Moros. The father and mother died before they
could be tortured to the point where they'd tell. They

bled to death with slashed wrists. That's the way the Moros found them when they sneaked back."

"But you said they'd been gagged and tied up. Did the Moros do the slashing before they left, knowing what might happen?"

Toni was bland. "How do I know? But I hear the bandages on the wrists were nice professional ones, with gauze that you don't see in a Moro hut."

"Tay?" The whisper was almost inaudible.

Toni shrugged. "Maybe he was nervous. Maybe his hand slipped twice when he was trying to bring 'em to, for questioning. Slipped with a knife instead of a hypo. And then maybe he tied those nice neat bandages to show the Japs his heart was in the right place, with dear old Nippon. And even being a doctor, maybe he was so jittery it didn't strike him that for severed arteries a tourniquet might be more useful than a bandage."

"A wonder the Nips didn't think of that."

"Oh, they did after a while. Someone tried to make crude tourniquets finally, but it was too late. It must have been about that time Tay got kicked around a bit—the polite compliments that kept him in the hospital later."

"Why didn't they kill him then and there?"

"Needed him at camp for their own men. Not a Nip doctor within two hundred miles, and what medical supplies they had or their prisoners had, they didn't know how to use . . . And that's the one and only reason Taynor Harrison is here for you to crab because he's taking it too personal!" Toni stared at Ester with a look that was almost stern. "I don't think it's just personal," he said harshly, "even if it was because of her he had to kill two decent people with his own hands to keep 'em from being killed more slowly, them and their boys. You might think a doctor wouldn't mind having to do that as much as someone else would. I think he'd mind it more. Then there was the little girl. Don't forget her."

"I don't." She lifted a weary hand. "And I've seen as bad or worse."

Toni threw her a swift compassionate look. "I know. What I'm driving at is that all those things happened together—to Tay. He was the only one of the prisoners who saw the little girl or the family because he was the only one the Nips needed. And he was the only one who was positive sure it was Yokohama Lily that they were using for a decoy. The other men heard her, the other prisoners, but they weren't sure like he was. Why? Because he was the only trained musician in the bunch."

"He's a pianist, not a singer."

"He's a concert pianist," Toni corrected patiently. "Just because you don't know *Old Black Joe* from *Pagliacci*, don't think he doesn't know. He's solo-ed and he's accompanied singers. He was a guest artist with the Boston Symphony at a charity affair. You don't like evidence turning on a song, on a phrase in a song. Because why? Because you wouldn't know whether it was sung right or not. Because most singing voices sound alike to you. Because, to put it in a nutshell, you're tone deaf." As Ester's face showed signs of an imminent explosion, he went on even more hastily though his eyes twinkled.

"Oh, you're a wow on all the rest. You read people like some birds read books, fast and accurate."

"I don't butter easy, so don't you try it, Toni Scaletti."

Her smile was reluctant as Toni squeezed her shoulder
with an unabashed arm. "If you were older I would have
you for a mother," he said. "As it is, I will just call you
my favorite aunt." His melting black eyes caressed her as
he added thoughtfully, "But never try to sing me to sleep."
He dodged expertly the blow she aimed at him, and strolling across to the table he stood looking down at the two
disks she had laid there.

"She hasn't sung for nearly a week?"

"No."

"How do you know?"

"Well, Tay said so and I haven't heard her."

"Doesn't prove she couldn't have slipped in here and
fooled around by herself. Hardly seems natural for a
singer not to."

"Listen," Ester said positively, "she never sings unless
she has to. She'd like to forget that she ever sang. But she
doesn't dare refuse Tay when he asks her, for fear he'd put
two and two together. And she thinks he's beginning to
do just that. He practically handed his suspicions to her
on a silver platter. You don't look surprised."

"I'm not. He's that sort. Just because he hates her guts
he'd lean over backward to give her an even break. Then
too, maybe he's hoping she'll get flustered enough to tip
her hand. Well, Washington has another line out if this
doesn't work." He kicked a needlepoint hassock gloomily.
"I wish to God he hadn't married her. Tay can rattle her
a bit but that's all. She's not the sort to have the scream-
ing meemies over anything or she'd be in a strait-jacket
now, with all that's on her mind. That is, if she has a
mind."

"Oh, she has one all right. But there's nothing to go with it. Where other people wear a heart, there's only something in her sort of like a jellyfish. You touch it but you can't see it. It slithers away, leaving you nothing but a rash to prove it was ever there."

Toni threw back his head and laughed, then he sobered. "Perhaps you can't blame her too much, if she was born like that."

"I do blame her." Ester was grim. "She isn't insane, unless one hundred percent selfishness is insanity. But there's always a time when selfishness hasn't hardened, so to speak. You still got a choice. And Iris must have had that choice once, at least, in the beginning." She glared at Toni. "You men are all alike. She's pretty, so already you're making excuses."

Toni threw out his hands in an inimitable Latin gesture. "Me? All I can do is smack my lips while Tay eats the dish."

"And vulgar too." Ester was really angry now and Toni was repentant. But he counterattacked.

"Who was telling you about her?" he demanded. "Who was speaking of the little girl? Listen, to sit down at the same table with that woman would turn my stomach."

"Tay feels the same way. If you could see him stare at her while he eats that rice every night—"

"Sure. On the other hand," Toni added with too transparent innocence, "there are rooms and rooms in a house, beside the dining room. That is all I point out." He changed the subject hastily as her frown gathered again. "If you think I needn't bother with the other records, I won't."

"They're the only ones Tay spoke of particularly."

"He's boss at the moment," Toni said, then winked. "At least he thinks so. Did you tell him about your promotion?"

"Why should I?" she said placidly. "He's a civilian now and it wouldn't matter to him one way or the other. I'm willing to follow along with him as long as there's any chance of his getting somewheres. Fact is, we just about have to. It'll be at least a week before we can pick up the other trail. And if we don't crack a few alibis, even that won't do much good."

The disks under his arm, Toni followed her from the room. "Are you staying on the whole time they're gone?"

She shook her head. "No. I have to meet a boat in Halifax next week."

He stared at her, grinned. "Well, good luck to us all. With two finesses, one ought to go through."

IT WAS QUIET here. It was all-enveloping yet somehow safe. Iris looked around her with real pleasure as she sat on the birch log that Karen had indicated. Already the trail itself seemed to have vanished though she was comfortably sure that Karen would have no difficulty in picking up the blazed trees that pointed the way back to the Lodge. Giant firs and pines and other trees she could not so easily identify huddled together here so closely that their majestic height was almost lost, for they absorbed the sky itself. They huddled so closely that when one of them crumbled under age or snow or lightning it must have sunk softly on the shoulders of its mates, with a muffled groan rather than a crash.

Only this tiny glade was open a bit to the sunlight. Through it a dark small brook ran, its passage silent between the shoulders of foot-thick green moss. The moss was crushed in spots, onyx pits welling mud where a bear had threaded an equally silent passage. Though she had yet to see a bear, Iris considered the fact of its existence placidly. Animal life was so harmless here, so timid: the brown soft deer, the maidenly beaver, the apologetic bear. For an instant the other day she had felt a swift kinship for the fox they had glimpsed, but it proved a kinship born of literary allusion rather than fact. For he had turned on the shoulder of the hill to stare at them, one paw uplifted as a dog might stand. His red and white fur was bushy against the coming winter, not sleek, so that the feel of his speed and alertness was lost. Nor was his look sly; it was wide and interested.

"Gun—gun!" Iris had shrieked. And it was only at the sound of her voice that he had turned and loped into the woods, with a dignity that had given it almost the illusion of a saunter. Not, one might say, a fox at all. She had felt a sense of annoyance, of contempt.

Only when she had seen the hoofprints of the moose had she felt any quiver of fear, a delicious quiver. The mighty head and antlers on the Lodge wall—one wouldn't care to meet those antlers. "How about the bull-moose?" she asked Karen idly. Karen had whisked off the top of the thermos with one slim brown hand, and now she was pouring Iris a paper cup of coffee. She turned an amused smile on her guest.

"Safe as a church. They'll never attack a human or almost never. For one thing, it's always a closed season on moose now and they seem to know it."

Iris was plaintive. "Almost never. Then it's happened."

"I've only known one case," Karen conceded. "Ben Jedder. And because he's a guide we have to keep it most frightfully dark. But he couldn't help it. It was in winter and he had crossed a lake and was entering a little ravine. Well, the moose was in the ravine too. It didn't have room to turn quickly so it had only the choice of leaping past Ben out to the lake ice, or of attacking him. Moose are afraid of an ice leap, their legs are so brittle. So it made for Ben and he had to shoot it in self-defense. He also had to keep the whole thing quiet because the wardens don't take any excuses from licensed guides. No, a moose won't attack as long as it sees any other possible road for escape."

"Any other possible road," Iris repeated, then fell silent again as they ate their sandwiches. She was remembering Marie Saulnier, Marie who had spoken of a possible road for escape. Iris had met Marie through Baron von Bohlen and for a time the three of them had seemed to move as one unit, sharing the same high plans, the same contemptuous laughter. Then Marie had flawed suddenly, at a moment when they had least expected it. Her diamond composure had cracked and her worth was seen as worthlessness; more than that, as danger. It had been a good thing for Marie that it had been Iris alone who had seen her at that moment.

"I can't go on, 'Ris," Marie had said abruptly. She had come into Iris' room, dressed for travel, only her small handbag gripped in her exquisitely gloved hand. "I'm leaving, going back to Paris. I'm only taking this bag. You can have everything I've left."

Iris' hairbrush had paused in midair, her eyes unbelieving on Marie. Her ears deliberately shut out the sound and clatter of the Tokyo street beneath her windows, the shrill din of a tramcar in the distance. She turned back to the mirror and the golden hair began to cascade again under the brush. "But you'll have to go on," she said. She reached out and pulled a bell rope. "Find the Scotch, will you? The ice will be up in a moment."

"It's no good," Marie said in a high voice that began to shake. "I'm not crazy, I'm not hysterical, I'm not going to have a drink. I'm going to go. I've decided."

And now Iris swung around on the low satined stool. "Why?"

"There are some things—too much."

"Since when?"

"Since last night. No, since weeks ago, I think."

Marie's sleek black hair was folded like wings about her ears and her face had the ravaged pallor of a small, decadent madonna. Iris picked up a cigarette, tapped it meditatively on one coral-tipped thumb. "Then you should have done it weeks ago," she pointed out. "It's too late now."

"It's never too late."

"Ah." Iris lit the cigarette, blew a small smoke ring. "A sudden attack of religion?"

Marie's eyes shifted, her full purple-red lips quivered. "No. At least I don't think so." Her clenched small fist struck her chest suddenly. "I'm afraid for my skin!" she whispered. "I'm afraid, I'm afraid! And maybe I'm afraid of other things too. You sleep," she accused, "you sleep all night long. I can't. Not any more."

Iris sighed. Already her mind was made up. No argument was possible here. Even if one mended this breakage temporarily, it would occur again and again. Marie was through. And unless one were very careful, Iris and Fritz would be through also. She spoke gently as one speaks to an unreasonable child. "Darling, I had no idea you were being so unhappy. Of course if you want to go, you must. But Fritz won't feel too pleased about this, you know. Neither will our honorable allies." Her mouth curled ironically. "And why Paris, of all places? Perhaps you've forgotten that Paris isn't French any longer."

"I hadn't forgotten. I know where to go. I'll be safe there."

"Where?"

Marie stared at Iris, held the latter's eyes with a terrible, pleading intensity. "Perhaps I'm foolish to tell you. But perhaps if I do you'll see that I won't be—that I *can't* be anyone for you to worry about."

"Well?"

"A third cousin of mine is Mother Superior in one of the convents outside Paris. They will take me in."

"You are not a Catholic."

"Like you, I am not anything. But I was baptized in the Church."

"And for those few drops of water you expect to be sheltered indefinitely?"

Marie said slowly, "No. But if I give everything I have to their charities and if I do faithfully my penances . . . there is always forgiveness some day if one repents—in time."

"You, a *nun?*" Iris' laugh rang out unrestrained now.

Marie recoiled from that laugh and her mouth set in stubborn lines. "No," she said again and there was an uncertain small dignity in her voice for the first time, "of course not. But there are lay workers."

"Where is the convent?"

Marie hesitated, visibly disturbed, but under the hard pressure of Iris' eyes she mumbled the name. Again Iris laughed. "My God, Marie, a poverty Order!"

Marie said passionately, "Poverty? What have I now? Fear, fear, fear! I cannot live under it! I am going slowly insane!"

"I think you're optimistic about what the Order will do for you," Iris said, but she was revolving the matter thoughtfully. At that, it might be possible for Marie to manage it. Iris was remembering a dog-eared copy of true murder trials that she had once picked up in a Maidan bazaar. There had been the story of a young English girl, Constance Kent, her name had been. (Iris nodded to herself with satisfaction for her excellent memory.) Constance had murdered her small brother, had been acquitted. But in a torment of conscience she had gone to a convent, confessed her crime and had lived there quietly for years, protected by the seal of the confessional, unmolested. Eventually that same conscience, constantly worked upon by her spiritual advisors, had brought her to the police with a public statement of her crime. But it had taken long years for that foolish weakness to show itself. And if Marie's years too were long enough, she need not be feared.

"And how do you expect to get to Paris?" she asked lazily.

"That I shall not tell you," Marie said with a sudden show of spirit, "for you might be forced to tell Fritz and he would try to stop me. But I tell you I will get there, I can get there. Arrangements are already made, if you will only say nothing to Fritz for at least two days."

Iris buffed her nails absently. "Why did you tell me at all?"

Marie sank on her knees beside Iris and her weak full mouth quivered. "I had hoped you would go with me," she whispered, "but I see now that was a foolish hope."

"Yes, it was foolish." The two stared at each other, then Iris tapped the girl's shoulder lightly. "I won't tell Fritz," she said. "I will know nothing of your departure and will ask no more questions."

"Oh, 'Ris, thank you!"

"But I think you will not need that diamond ring, eh? Consider me as your first most deserving charity."

Marie drew back, staring at Iris. Then she rose to her feet, pulled off the ring and laid it on the dressing table (so occidental in its fluting of maidenly chintz). Without speaking again she left the room, a small blackbird whose wings were already beginning to lose their sheen, already touched by the caged future. Iris had enjoyed her Scotch alone, turning the diamond over and over in her hand.

Blackbird . . . woods. Iris was back in the woods again, finishing a sandwich whose edges were curling with dryness. In this muted, murmurous quiet a vista had suddenly opened before her, a vista so strange, so straight, so crystal-clear that she stared into it with an almost wild amazement. Actually, it was still not too late to do as Marie had done. It should not be too difficult to vanish into this Canada, to go to some quiet French-Canadian convent, to turn over her money together with her past; and sink into the anonymity of being a lay worker.

There would be a thousand tedious steps of course— convent years in Paris had taught her that, and not the least tedious would be that necessary "conversion"; as though she had anything to convert *from*, she thought with hard amusement. There would be severe penances for years (the hair stirred at the back of her neck), there would be a lifetime of self-denial and backbreaking toil. But she would be safe. An alien voice deep inside her said pressingly, *and others would be safe.* Never mind those

others now; it would be Iris whose name and identity
would slip as soundlessly into the stream of the future as
that detached bit of moss had slipped into the brook and
been whirled away. Eventually her past would wash away
with every pail of water, every scrubbing brush—

She made a stifled sound in her throat and Karen turned.
"What's the joke?"

"I didn't laugh. I was thinking that the moose knew
the ice but he didn't know Ben Jedder, so naturally he
took what he thought was the best chance." She added
with a curious harshness, "Why didn't Ben back out, get
out of the way?"

Karen folded the wax paper neatly and thrust it back
into the box. "I suppose the moose didn't give him time."
She stood up. "Do you want to prowl with me or would
you rather have your cigarette here?"

"Here, I think. I'm lazy." Her eyes glinted up at
Karen. "And don't remind me about the stub. I'll see
it's well doused in the moss." Karen moved away, as slim
and brown and quiet as any deer. Only her eyes were not
like a deer's, Iris thought. For once, and strangely enough,
there was no rancor in her idle contemplation of Karen.
Karen's eyes were mischievous and alert. But sometimes
lately they held quietness and a question. Iris knew what
that question was, and now she turned it over and over in
her mind with a sort of detached speculation. Karen wondered if she, Karen, were in love with Tay. Very soon she
would know and then there would be a new question in
those eyes. And sometime—very suddenly and without pre-
meditation—Tay would see the question and know that he
held the answer . . .

Iris ground the stub into the moss, but her foot was gentle. Her mood was dispassionate for she was still contemplating that vista, almost with an open mind. Karen had vanished, and around her was only the rising of the afternoon wind and the faint dank smell of moss and peeling birch bark. A bar of thin October sunlight struck down in front of her and in it she watched the gnats dance their sad vertical dance of death. No longer swarming in rapturous summer circles, they moved endlessly up and down the escalator of that sunray, their last flutters of life restricted to a narrowing bar of autumn light. A thin meager light, void of warmth and color. A light that was a mockery and a treadmill for the feet of death. A convent.

"No," she said aloud. "No. Marie could. I could not."

With the sound of her own voice the whole glade seemed to come alive to her ears, or perhaps in the unwonted silence her hearing had become more acute. Now she could hear the faint cracklings of the underbrush, even distinguish the brook's sound where it ran beneath the fallen log and slapped a boulder softly. She felt a relieved glow run through her whole body as though her feet had drawn back at the very brink of some terrifying and unknown land.

Safe, she toyed luxuriously with the reminiscence of her escape. But already the former moment, the former mood had eluded her, like a dream that vanishes as one attempts to seize it. She could still see the absurd picture but it was blank of meaning; a crude canvas with which her imagination, usually predictable, had affronted her. It had been the woods, she thought with amusement, the first strange woods she had ever been in that seemed friendly. They had made her sentimental, maudlin.

Karen came through the bushes. She was frowning a little. "Sorry," she said, "I'd hoped to take you on a new trail we just blazed last year, but a fallen tree has blocked it. And I'm afraid crossing the swamp to go 'round would be too rough for you until you've had a bit more experience. We'll have to go back the same way."

"I don't mind going back the same way," Iris said. She smiled, thinking that Karen's remark had capped most neatly her own meditation. There was a new trail but it had been blocked. Selah, amen, and so-be-it. How long ago had the tree fallen? For a really spectacular analogy it should have fallen but a little time before, at the moment when her common sense had asserted itself over a queer impulse: an impulse so foreign that it had almost seemed thrust upon her from some external source, some genie of the woods perhaps. "When did it fall?" she asked.

Karen yawned. "Oh, last winter probably. You needn't be afraid of a tree beaning you at this season, except in a lightning storm." Karen's face was flushed with her rapid walk. She had pushed the red scarf back from her head and one small dark curl had fallen over her forehead. Beneath the black lashes her eyes had a soft brightness, an impersonality. Iris stared at her. The woods were not so friendly after all. In them, Karen drew away, Tay drew away, even Gregory drew away. Not to each other exactly, but into the woods themselves. They stepped into some medium and were gone. As Iris stared, a faint frown gathered between her eyes and the pendulum of her mind began to swing again through its familiar arc, a swing more relentless for the pause that had held it static those brief moments.

"May I lead the way this time?" she asked. "It's so tiresome always following someone else."

"Of course. En avant!"

Iris walked the trail well, Karen noted with approval. Her footing was sure and her eye keen for the quickest, easiest passage over fallen branch or deceptive bog or slippery pine carpet. Presently they were making their way through the only unpleasant part of the trail, a copse of saplings so crowded together that the eye must be constantly alert for a treacherous twig; saplings still so vigorous with sap that an unguarded movement might bring a small shower of whiplashes about one. They were almost out of the copse when Iris plunged forward in an unusually brusque motion, thrusting and holding back a long green branch.

She waited until Karen was almost at her heels, then with a negligent "You have it?" she stepped forward, releasing the branch as she spoke. Karen's own arm had not been quick enough. She made a stifled sound as the heavy bough struck her full across the breast, grazing her chin. Iris swung around immediately.

"M'Dieu! Didn't you have hold of it? Oh, my dear, I'm terribly sorry!"

Karen stepped clear of the copse. "It's all right," she said cheerfully. "Fortunately I'm taller than you are or I'd have had it right across the eyes." She patted the long angry welt on her chin with her handkerchief. "No damage done to speak of, but I'd have hated to have it land across the old orbs." Iris fluttered about with little excla-

mations of abject apology until Karen burst out laughing.
"My dear woman, this chin scratch isn't anything and my
skin heals so easily that I never get any sympathy. Lead
on."

But her look was thoughtful as she followed Iris up the
last slope toward the portage. Karen had long ago discovered with some inner amusement and occasional anguish
that she was naturally credulous. But she hadn't lived in
crowded quarters in Africa with various types of women
for over a year without learning a few things. Iris wasn't
clumsy. She had a keen eye and a sure hand; for that matter, a strong hand for all its delicate whiteness. Karen
could have sworn that little accident had been deliberate.
No, she wouldn't have sworn it; she only knew it, as surely
as she knew her chin was beginning to smart painfully.
But even such trivial malice must have some provocation.
Jealousy? Of what? Of—whom? The answer was swift because it was the only answer. But if that were so, then
. . . Karen stumbled and Iris turned.

"Don't sprain your ankle too," she admonished lightly.
"I won't take the blame for any more accidents."

Karen said just as lightly, "Has anyone been blaming
you?"

"Oh, but they will. As soon as Tay and Greg see your
chin they'll rush to get out the medicine chest."

"I doubt it. But don't begrudge me a little attention."
Karen thoroughly enjoyed the bland cattiness of her own
retort.

"Oh, as long as it's *medi*cal, pet—" Iris' laugh was warm.

"And as long as it's *Greg*ory." Karen's smile was equally
warm and a good deal more steady. A pine cone plopped

near by. As though the sound had been a tiny curtain signal, Karen drew out a cigarette package, offered it to Iris and lit the two cigarettes. Iris inhaled a long breath of smoke and felt a heady excitement that wasn't nicotine induced. The game was going to be even more interesting. A credulous Karen had posed a problem, not in scruples but in tactics; but there was evidently nothing of simpleness beneath Karen's simplicity. And with this woman who eyed her so steadily and pleasantly Iris found herself on familiar battle ground when she had least expected it. Karen's eyes above the match flame hadn't held a question any longer; they had been lazy, appraising. Iris nodded to herself with satisfaction and stepped out upon the portage. The two women walked up it, talking easily, volubly.

Back in the deep woods the ray of sunlight still hung, but narrower, fainter now. And the gnats still danced their sad vertical dance. Time and light seemed synonymous and eternal, even while the space of their jauntiness closed in upon them.

9

A<small>T THE</small> L<small>ODGE</small>, Karen and Iris paused by mutual consent on the wooden porch that ran along its length; terrace rather than porch, for it was roofless. One could perch on the rail and from this vantage point survey miles of the river that ran below them, hurrying to join the Mirimichi. The Lodge had been built on the highest point of the bluff, where the river bank rose a good hundred feet above the channel. The bluff was at its steepest angle here too. Years ago the serpentine wooden steps that had once been placed there, had rotted away; and now only an occasional hardy guide chose to scramble a precarious ascent at this point rather than take an easier way farther along the bluff. Even that latter climb meant a sure foot and considerable agility in seizing handholds, so that Gregory had cheerfully dubbed the Lodge, the Goat Club. He himself was forced to go to and from the river at a spot a good quarter-mile down the portage, where the bluff sloped to an innocuous angle.

But if the location of the Lodge entailed some inconvenience for the fishermen, it assured a view unsurpassed for miles around. Behind them and across the river the untouched forests rose and north and west they marched in unbroken continuity to the St. Lawrence. Even east or south the nearest village was a good two and a half hours by weary truck drive down the portage. The latter, which colloquial usage had long ago corrupted to "potash," was road more by courtesy than fact for a good part of its length. It was used only during the few weeks annually when the Lodge was open, and even less frequently by the lumber company that had been given the right of passage through this private preserve. Deliberately, the Littlefields had allowed the portage to remain uninviting to the possible trespasser or poacher.

So the road had never been trammeled into conventional ways. Its ruts were apt to sink suddenly into bogs that could engulf the axle of a ten-ton truck with indifference. Or it might choose to move aside affably for the benefit of a new creek. Or again it would offer whole stretches of terrain that could imaginatively be called a highway. It was gracious to the pedestrian, allergic to any motor vehicle lighter than a truck, accepted the great horse-drawn wagons of the lumberman with a philosophy born of necessity. The guides, to whom the portage represented civilization itself after weeks in the trackless woods, felt a reverent fondness for its temperamental length. And from the Lodge they bicycled the twelve miles to the village with apparent aplomb. It was not considered good taste for Lodge visitors to seem aware of the fact that for at least seven of those miles a bicycle must be pushed, not ridden.

Now as Karen looked down the portage she saw her father coming along it. He carried her bird gun, and the pouch hanging from his shoulder was heavy with partridge. She exclaimed contritely. One of her duties was keeping the great outdoor meatbox supplied with partridge when it was wanted. "I forgot all about it," she said. "Well, he couldn't have had any luck with deer, so it's just as well I

gave him the chance for a shot or two. But going after
birds bores him stiff." She glanced down the river and
sat up alertly. "Look, Iris! Greg has a strike. A honey
too, by the way he's fighting."

Far down the river and far below them, they could see
two miniature figures, foreshortened, standing in mid-
stream. The air was crystal, with no shimmering heat
waves to blur the picture. Karen ran into the house and
reappeared with the field glasses. "Watch them," she said
and handed the glasses to Iris. And Iris watched as Gregory battled the big fish, as he backed step by step toward
the shore; watched as the air exploded in a silver flash a
good six feet above the water and as Ben, from the boat-
side, gaffed the salmon. Iris laid down the glasses. Now
that the small drama was over, Gregory and Ben were just
two men absurdly standing in freezing water.

"It must be fun playing them," she conceded, "but I'm
sure I'd lose my head if I actually hooked one. And as for
gaffing it—ugh!" She shrugged prettily.

Still, it was peaceful and oddly pleasant out here at this
present hour. From somewhere in the servants' quarters
a radio was playing faintly and the sound only emphasized
their isolation from the outside world. She looked with a
faint envy at Karen; Karen, the tenor of whose life was
broken only by such weeks as these, one picture of peace
replaced by another. Yet even this peace had its small
death, she mused: death for the partridge, death for the
salmon, death for the deer. How hypocritical people were,
shuddering away from pain and oblivion when it was in-
flicted on their own kind; yet conferring that oblivion on

another species as an integral part of their own vacation pleasure.

Pain and death were facts, whatever the species that had to accept them. That being the case, what was the difference between her, Iris, and the Littlefields and Tay—and Marie? Nothing, except that they postulated a human soul. Well, she did not. She did not accept their premises; she was consequently not forced to accept their conclusions, as her father would have pointed out.

The mood of the whole group was lazy that evening, and no one was inclined for cards when the dishes had been cleared from the table that stood in an alcove of the great living room. Karen had vanished for a determined overhauling of the storage room. It hadn't been touched since before the war, she had declared, and had spoken darkly of moths, mice and porcupine. This, despite the fact that the boxes were swung in wire cages from pulleys in the ceiling.

Their feet on the low rail of the huge stove, the three men argued amiably the question of the respective areas over which they would hunt the next day. By the stove hung a slate on which would be scrawled the final decisions. Just as no gun except bird gun could be carried loaded within a certain area around the Lodge, so it was an unalterable rule that each hunter keep to his own section, a section clearly stated on the slate each day. Gregory rose and stared at the calendar. "Hey, only five more days of the fishing season! You can take my section too, Dad," he declared. "I'm for the river again tomorrow."

Under the big kerosene lamp, Iris knitted sedately. Her

physical relaxation was complete but beneath it still ran
an uneasy stir of perturbation. Perhaps it was an echo of
that queer suspended moment in the woods when she had
actually contemplated throwing her life away, as one
might throw a discarded scrap of paper into the fire. It
disturbed her that her mind could have taken such an
absurd lurch from its beaten path, that her disciplined
sureness should have disintegrated even for a second. Or
perhaps it was an echo of her panic that night on the
train nearly a week ago, panic about a possible walled-in
room, she remembered now. She had tracked that panic
down, had been about to examine it—when Tay had
spoken from the bunk above.

The needles in her hands stilled. Beneath her absorp-
tion she was aware of Gregory's slow circling of the room
toward her. From calendar to the table in the corner;
from a listless glance into a magazine to an aimless toying
with the radio which stood near her. Dance music blared
loudly, and as though the noise had conferred some cloak
of invisibility on him, Gregory abandoned all pretense and
coming to her he seated himself on a hassock near by.

"Just in time," she said. "Hold out your hands, I want
to wind some more yarn." Their faces were near together
now and the music was loud. Loud enough, she knew, for
the conversation of Tay and Judge Littlefield had become
inaudible. This time she would not allow herself to be
sidetracked. This time her thoughts would follow the
thread to the end of the maze. For there was a maze here
somewhere. Her instinct, her trouble sense, was too strong
to be disregarded.

Gregory said, "Radio too noisy? Want me to turn it

down?" It was the *Danse Macabre* now, and the violin was scraping its first antic chords.

She shook her head. "No. If you do we'll miss some of the quieter parts. If you were in a concert hall you'd have to take it at that volume." She added, "But I'm glad the music room at home seems to build up sound without assaulting the ears. It's a lovely room, don't you think? But somehow it doesn't belong with the rest of the house. You know, I believe that originally it wasn't a music room at all, that it was bigger, another drawing room perhaps."

Gregory looked puzzled. "But of course it was," he said. "Tay had the room practically rebuilt. The whole thing was ripped out and made over from A to Z. I'll bet it has finer acoustics than you'd find in any private home in the east. And it ought to have," he laughed, "with carpenters and electricians fussing over it for almost as long as they'd have taken to build a whole house. I hope you made the proper noises of thanks for your special wedding present."

Iris' hands paused in midair, then continued winding the yarn. "Now you've snarled it," he commented. He moved his thumb, caught the yarn.

"Sorry." After a moment, "I'm afraid I didn't make any noises at all, let alone properly appreciative ones," she said thoughtfully. "You see, this is the first time I knew Tay had the room done over himself."

Gregory bit his lip ruefully. "Have I put my foot in it?"

She laughed. "Not at all. I imagine that Tay had it remodeled for himself originally, for his own work. Then when he found I sang a bit he wanted me to feel free to use it as much as I wanted. Perhaps I wouldn't have felt

so free if I'd known it was to have been his private sanc-
tum. Perhaps he knew that and that's why he didn't tell
me."

Gregory was alarmed. "You're not going to get some
silly notion that you should leave the room all to Tay?
Why didn't I keep my big mouth shut! But I had no idea
he hadn't told you all about it. Please, Iris. He'll never
forgive me."

"Don't tell him you told me," she advised lightly, "and
I won't tell either. And don't worry. I'll sing as much as
I ever do, but I'll also see to it that Tay spends a good
many more hours in there by himself than he's been doing.
It's ridiculous that he went to all that bother and expense
unless the room is used more than it is now. I doubt if
I'm in there an hour a week."

"Give him time."

"He's had quite enough time," Iris said. When she
spoke again her voice was casual, disinterested. "Did
Karen boss the construction job too? Heaven knows she
did everything else in connection with the house."

Gregory grinned. "Boss it? She wasn't even allowed
near it! No one was. The day I innocently sauntered
over, some Italian electrician was there with all his men.
He practically shot me when I came up on the terrace.
Must have thought I looked like a hard character and
wasn't taking any chances, what with the owner being
abroad. I suppose at that," Gregory added comfortably,
"he was responsible for the house while he was working
there, and couldn't let any casual stranger just wander in
and poke around. Particularly in a furnished place."

"*All* his men?" Iris raised her eyebrows. "Is wiring for one room such a job?"

"Well, there were only two or three. But I don't know a thing about acoustics," Gregory admitted frankly. "Maybe you have to have electricians put amplifiers or something in the ceiling. Or do acoustics just depend on the architectural shape of a room, and the proper draperies?"

"I wouldn't know," Iris said.

But she did know. It seemed now that she had known since that moment when she had paused on the stairs and looked into the hall mirror. And now her obsession and the reality had fused. Tay had had the room built. It followed that he had also planned that hidden space. It wouldn't be an empty space, any more than a control room in a studio is an empty space. It would have a machine, that space, and it would have wiring that ran cunningly concealed beneath the rugs to the piano. Perhaps overhead too.

Even as far back as Lisbon, then, even a few days after their marriage, Tay had begun to guess. He hadn't been sure, but he had guessed. How? For she had never spoken over the radio, or only that once; nor had she ever sung for him until she arrived in America. Back there in Lisbon he had had only the memory of a singing voice to compare with the actuality of a speaking voice. Yet he had made the comparison. He had gambled on that comparison heavily enough to have had the music room built and the recording room concealed. (In her mind it was still, as always, the "control room.") It had been her first major bad luck that in Tay were combined a ruthless

mind, a gambler's instinct and a faultless ear; an ear as
sensitive in its receptivity as her own vocal chords were accurate in their production of absolute pitch . . .

Old Ben Jedder shambled into the room with his usual
armful of logs, and dropped them on the zinc hearth
with the usual shattering crash. In the woods his feet
stepped high and softly. Soundlessly he approached deer
and partridge and bear. But in the Lodge his incomings
and outgoings were always heralded by a series of crash-
ings, thumps and shufflings. Iris was vaguely aware that
Ben had embarked on one of his tall stories, that someone
had turned the radio off, that the others were facing expectantly toward her. The story, then, was being told for
her benefit. The smile came mechanically to her face.
Glancing down she saw with a mild surprise that the
winding must have been finished at some moment past,
for the ball of yarn lay in her lap.

"It was just a little small bear, Mrs. Harrison," Ben was
saying with a gleam in his black and ancient eyes, "so I
seen no reason to leave her there like I'd of had to if she'd
been bigger. So having no gun with me I smacked her one
with the blunt end of the ax, right in the head. And being
sure she was deader'n a doornail, I takes her outta the
trap. Well, now, what was I to do? I tell you what I did.
I takes off my belt—happen I was wearing an extry long
one—and I straps that bear to my back. Her back to my
back, so's her legs wouldn't be waving over my soljers.
She was a little small bear, like I said. Well, now, after
trampin' in that deep snow a time I gets clean tuckered
out. I lean against a tree for a few minutes to get my
breath. I'm not swearin' I didn't take a little nap, like.

Well, Mrs. Harrison, when I open my eyes, what do I see?" He paused expectantly and the pause, rather than the words, prompted Iris.

"Well?" she asked and her smile widened, fixed, knowing that she had heard nothing but a jumble of sound, knowing only that her mind was still racing, racing, racing on that inner quest.

"This is what I see! I look down and there is the ground thirty feet below me. I look around and there is a partridge almost sitting on my elbow. I look up and there is the top of the tree comin' closer, faster'n I like the look of. See what happened? See? That damn little small bear hadn't been dead at all! She'd come to and was a-climbin' that tree as fast as Harry-come-hither! And me bein' strapped to her, I was travelin' too. Don't talk to me about them parytroopers, Mrs. Harrison! Never did a parytrooper see the ground shootin' away from him instead of comin' up to hit him. Well, so you are askin', why am I here? I tell you why. Because I think quick, pull my knife and cut the belt! It was a good belt too."

Ben grinned toothlessly and triumphantly. "That's why I wear a stout rope to my pants now. Be goddam if any little small bear is ever goin' to ruint a good belt on me again!"

"Wasn't it rather a long fall to the ground?" Gregory asked callously. But Judge Littlefield's intervention saved the day. A half water glass of straight whisky appeared as from nowhere and Ben accepted it with a surprised flourish; though it was a miracle that occurred regularly twice a week. He cackled, his face a network of wrinkles as brown and ingrained as bark. He tossed the whisky off in one sustained breath and ambled happily from the room. They had all laughed hearty, he nodded to himself, but Mrs. Harrison had laughed the heartiest. The new lady hadn't heard it before, of course. Not that a good story lost by retelling. In fact, to Ben's mind, it was only by the tenth or twelfth repetition that a story began to take on the fine richness and solidity that should dignify it.

Iris' hands still moved with apparent purpose among the yarns.

Very well, so Tay had planned to record her singing voice, probably had recorded it time and again. But what good would it do him? Even if his records were compared with recordings taken from her broadcasts, nothing could result but still more guesswork, a conflict of opinion. One could hear the same aria recorded by various singers and still doubt, still guess as to their identities. In trained singing there were not even the differentiations, the personal mannerisms that mark the conversational voice.

It was true that instinctively she had evaded singing *Home, Sweet Home* for Tay. It was too intimately associated with a period which she had firmly put behind her. It was true that her first real suspicion of Tay had crystallized when he had asked her to sing it—and he had only asked once. Or had that been the first moment of real fear? Had there actually been any such moment until this present one? She had thought so once, but as compared with her reaction when Gregory had spoken, those early suspicions of Tay had been weak and nebulous. Something to consult occasionally, but in the main, something to ignore until such time as further events confirmed or disputed them.

Well, those suspicions had been confirmed. But there was still no reason for fear, no reason for her wrists to feel so weak. Nothing had been changed except to her advantage. Only her knowledge had been broadened, not Tay's. He was obviously as far from his objective as he had been when he had first ordered the music room built. Otherwise she wouldn't be here now, vacationing, secure, entertained by his good friends. Her position was, in fact, strengthened. For now she knew, now she was better armed. She could smile at the music room, at the recording room with its ambush of dictaphones as stagey as any that might dot an Oppenheim novel. So far, Tay had failed. He knew it. He had angrily confessed his failure that night on the train when he had refused to share her berth. No, he had confessed it those nights before when he had been away "on business." He had simply taken a room in town to avoid entering the conjugal chamber at home. So before they left for Canada he had finally realized the recording business was a washout. That, in reality, was the reason why they were here. Tay had needed this change, this recess from her, to face his failure.

For the first time in an hour a spontaneous smile edged Iris' mouth. She wasn't foolish enough to believe that Tay's own convictions about her had swerved, and certainly there hadn't been any change in his attitude to indicate it; no halt to those small darts of innuendo that he constantly hurled at her from behind his blandness. But he was angry, angry that his hope of proof had fallen through. For a time his courage had failed and he had not been able to keep up the pretense of sharing her room.

But he was logical. And that logic of his would work to her advantage eventually if she only kept her head.

He was a scientist. He worked with facts, with proof. If facts and proof continually evaded him he would begin to doubt his own intuition, would weaken, would rationalize; would, in the end, ascribe his whole theory to an insanity born of war suffering and war weariness. And her physical hold on him would hasten that process. Even if for the time being he recoiled from her, she had held him once, many times. And in each of those small desperate surrenders he had weakened still more the citadel he held against her. The citadel would fall finally, it would be hers if she wanted it. She looked thoughtfully across at Judge Littlefield. She might not want Tay's citadel permanently. His malehood, his strength challenged her now, excited her; a citadel in rubble would bore her.

But about the music room . . . perhaps it would be useful to develop a bad throat that would linger indefinitely after they returned home. No, she thought, that would be silly and unconvincing. And it didn't matter what Tay thought, now that she knew he could prove nothing.

No one could prove anything.

There were only two people in the world who had ever known that Iris O'Hearn and the Yokohama Lily were one and the same person. One of those two people, Fritz von Bohlen, had been in Hiroshima on a certain August day in 1945. Exit, the Baron, most finally. The other was Marie Saulnier, now presumably immured for life in a Parisian convent. Iris considered the question of Marie thoughtfully. It might be wise to take a little trip to Paris one of these days. No, it wouldn't be wise, it would

be extremely foolhardy. Marie couldn't know whether
Yokohama Lily were alive or dead. No one could know.
And in every likelihood Marie was so buried under her
own personal fears, her own ritualistic penances and
drudgeries that she would feel no compulsion to confess
another's derelictions. Marie was a coward but she wasn't
stupid. How could she gain anything by betraying Iris?
In this avatar, Marie was only a lay worker crawling
through the days with one gasping hope, that her past
would one day be shrouded in a dusty obscurity. To speak
of Iris would be only to bring that past into glaring and
contemptible focus again. Moreover, if Marie hadn't
taken such a step during the furor and hysteria that characterized the war crimes' trials, she was hardly likely to do
so now that the world was again trying to go about its
everyday business.

Iris sat back with a little sigh of genuine relief. It
wouldn't have been pleasant to have taken Marie out to a
small café, to have had to put anything into her drink,
whatever the necessity. Cafés, drinks? What was she
thinking of! In all probability Iris would have been fortunate if she had been permitted to speak briefly with
Marie through some small grating, with a Sister standing
near-by. One could hardly push a chemist's paper through
such a grating and say, "Pardon me, Marie, but would
you be so good as to take this harmless tonic with your
next meal?"

Iris laughed aloud and Gregory looked up from his
magazine, smiling in sheer delight at that small musical
sound. "May I share it?"

"No, it's too silly. I was thinking of a dear old school

friend and some of our pranks when we were very young."

"Did you ever really prank?" Karen asked interestedly. She had just come into the room, bearing a large tissue-wrapped package which she now proceeded to lay tenderly on the table. "I can't imagine you as a schoolgirl at all. For that matter," she added hastily, "I can't imagine you as an old lady either . . . Look here, Tay. You won't have any difficulty remembering, let alone imagining, the time when I was ten."

Tay went over to the table and Iris too stood up, stretching herself as a cat stretches. She had been prisoner of the chair and her sickly thoughts far too long. "What is it?" she asked lazily as Karen unwrapped the package.

"My pet doll," Karen said triumphantly. "I thought she'd been thrown out long ago. But here she is as good as new. Or almost as good," she added on a more rueful note. "The elastic is quite gone, I'm afraid." It was a jointed bisque doll, with porcelain head, waxen eyelids and bleached human hair. Its pink and white were untarnished by time but as Karen had noted, the elastic that held its joints together had rotted with age; so now, instead of holding it up for admiration, she left it lying outstretched on the table.

"Look but don't touch," she warned. "But isn't she cute? And in perfect condition. All she needs is new elastic. Some youngster will cherish her as I did."

Against the warning, Iris' hand went out swiftly. "Pretty yellow hair," she said, "but I always liked curls on my dolls instead of pigtails." Her head closed possessively on a braid.

"Look out!" Karen exclaimed quickly. It was too late.

With a gentle little bisque clatter, the neck detached itself from the doll's body. The head tilted, and with the
momentum of Iris' yank on the braid, made a half-roll that
put inches between itself and the rest of its small cadaver.
As it tilted, the waxen eyelids lifted, gave Iris a brief glassy
blue gaze, then closed again. The head came to a rest
against Tay's hand, one yellow braid still stretched across
the table toward Iris' releasing hand.

Iris looked at the head and a frown of concentration, of
dawning uneasiness, creased her smooth face. Something
. . . there was something wrong. The head should have
been somewhere else. Yellow braids and a ditch . . . the
smell and the sound of death . . . And now her mouth
sagged as full and devastating memory swept in. She
looked up and met Tay's eyes. They were naked with
memory too, naked with a ferocious and unrelenting hate.
Yet his voice was soft enough, and his hand was immobile
under the small porcelain cheek that rested so quietly
against it.

"This is where I came in, Iris," he said.

She stared at him, literally unable to move her glance
from the blazing glare of his eyes. So Tay knew about—
that. Perhaps he had even been there. Among the prisoners there had been an American doctor, she remembered
now. She hadn't paid too much attention at the time, the
whole matter had been so distasteful, so messy . . . Yet she
could still hope.

"Only those other braids were still warm," Tay added
meditatively.

Her heart surged in her breast, floundered, made a

twisting leap as a salmon leaps against the death-dealing air in a final silver shower of despair and horror.

"Catch her, Greg!" Karen commanded sharply as Iris' head lolled back on her shoulders, but Greg's frantic arms had already moved, were supporting the woman's inert body, easing it to the floor.

Tay picked up the doll's head, placed it back in the tissue wrappings with careful precision. "I'll get the spirits of ammonia," he said quietly. And left the room.

But Iris was already conscious again. From the floor she looked up into Gregory's solicitous face with blank, drowning eyes.

K AREN CAME out to the porch, seated herself quietly on the top step beside Tay. The moon was climbing and the river lay seemingly shrunken between its banks, for its courses that bordered the shore were obscure, and only its center current flashed like a bright steel whip under the night sky.

She had waited until Iris was presumably asleep under the medicament Gregory had administered at Tay's suggestion. Or if Iris were not asleep, at least the creamy smoothness of her eyelids had not quivered as Karen had tiptoed out. After his wife had been tucked into her bed Tay had glanced in. He had made some perfunctory remark to her, then tapping Greg's shoulder he had said casually, "Your patient, I think," and had disappeared.

Gregory in his concern had seemed to find nothing remarkable about that, and perhaps if Gregory had been a full-fledged medico there would have been nothing remarkable. It wasn't customary for a physician to prescribe for his family if there were another doctor immediately available. But Gregory wasn't a doctor, he was a second-year student. Of course Tay had done the actual prescribing, Karen corrected herself. Even so he had left Iris entirely to Gregory's and Karen's care.

Karen knew why and the knowledge had shaken her, still shook her so that her palms were moist and cold. When that brief scene had taken place at the table, Gregory had been standing in such a position that he could not possibly have seen the interchange of glance between Tay and Iris; and Judge Littlefield had been deep in his paper by the stove. But Karen had seen. She had stood at the end of the table as the mutilated doll lay between those two, had seen the unmistakable terror in Iris' eyes, the even more unmistakable look in Tay's. That look of his had been hate—stark, naked hate.

Karen's first reaction to his look had not been one of exultation, even though in one brief quarter-hour that afternoon she had had to face two realizations: that she distrusted Iris, that she cared too much about Tay. She was glad to remember now that her distrust had been born first; that it was clean, distilled from a willow branch and a false note in Iris' voice; that it had not been a rationalization hurrying on the heels of her emotional turmoil about Tay. That distrust had struck her as surely and breathtakingly as the branch had struck her breast, her chin. If there had been no Taynor Harrison, if there had been only the two of them, two women alone in the woods, she would still have had that revelation, known that instant wary contempt for Iris.

Yet she had not been glad when she had seen Tay's eyes. She had felt an anguish that had its wellspring, not in fear for Iris but in fear for him. Whatever the source of his hatred, it could wreck him. But where its roots lay, where the solution might be, she did not know.

Her father had gone to bed, Gregory had gone to bed. And in those long moments before she had heard Tay's steps on the porch, heard him seat himself, she had lingered in the living room, thinking desperately, casting back over each look, trying to remember the words that had been spoken. They had been simple, innocuous enough. "This is where I came in—" that worn catch phrase. And a casual comment about some braids, some other braids presumably suggested by sight of the doll. Whose braids? Why? What could there be in those commonplace words that Iris should have lost consciousness under their impact, under the impact of Tay's stare?

She knew what Gregory had assumed as the cause of Iris' fainting spell, or at least what his first thought had been; for beneath his resigned tenderness had been a lack of any real anxiety. Whether Iris or Tay had disabused him of that natural yet false assumption, Karen didn't know; at the moment she didn't care. She would think about Gregory later. She had dreaded to join Tay, yet it must be done. So now she sat down beside him quietly.

He turned to her, struck the dottle from his pipe. "Iris asleep?"

"Yes."

"I'm afraid you—saw."

"Yes."

He stared ahead of him into the impenetrable gloom of the woods. "I've made a mess of things. I had no right to bring her into your life, to bring you people into ours."

Karen clasped her knees with her hands, said simply, "I wish I could help. But I'm lost, I haven't any clue."

"Naturally. I had thought maybe I could talk to you about it, about her, but I find I can't."

"No," she said thoughtfully, "I can see that."

He turned to her now, put a hard tense hand on hers

as they lay clasped on her knee. "Why do you accept the fact that I can't talk to you about Iris? Why?"

"I suppose because it isn't done," she said composedly enough, "to talk to another woman about one's wife, I mean."

"To talk to a *particular* woman about one's wife," he corrected. "To talk to *you* about Iris." His voice was low, savage. And now it was said. Her breath caught in her throat. But again Karen felt no exultation, only a deep sadness. She looked around, thinking how the hour, the night, the wildness of the scenery were stage-setting this moment as, since adolescence, she had hoped it would be set. But the night was an empty jewel box. The jewel was still there perhaps, but it rolled on the ground, trampled by the surge of feet as Tay and Iris interlocked above it in deadly combat. She, Karen, could only stand by wringing her hands. Even Tay took note of what he accidentally trampled only to mention it casually like this, almost as an aside.

"Let's walk down the portage. It's too early to sleep," he said. She nodded assent, almost listlessly. "Will you be warm enough?" For she had changed from her usual woolen slacks to the brief skirt and light sweater she wore during the evenings by the fire.

"It's the warmest night we've had since we've been here. But my coat is in a chair by the stove if you'll get it." For the evening had a mistral balminess and the light haze gathering around the moon indicated that the next day might bring either rain or some of those Indian-summer hours that even here in the north punctuated the normal tartness of the weather. "It could be eighty tomorrow,"

Karen added dreamily. Nevertheless Tay brought her top-
coat.

They walked down the portage, walked into that first
darkness where even the moon did not penetrate. The
road was dry here, but the ruts rose formidably, making
individual Indian trails for each pair of feet. From season
to season there was never a familiar pattern for the portage itself, but there was a familiar pattern for walking
it in the darkness. As she had held her father's hand,
Greg's hand and Tay's hand in those long past years, so
now Karen felt neither strangeness nor pleasure when
Tay's palm sought and found hers in the darkness. Their
arms swung in the free rhythm of their walk.

"We'll see the moon again when we come out at the
meadow."

"Yes."

"You're making it difficult for me to say anything to you,
Karen."

"Talk if you like, but I don't want to ask questions."

"You did nothing else but, when you were a child. And
ever since I've been back, there've been plenty of questions. Why don't I start medical practice again? Why
don't I get back to the piano? Why am I loafing, what's
eating me? Oh, you've asked plenty of questions!" Tay's
laugh was short but his hand tightened on hers as he felt
her fingers curl away from his. "Yet now tonight when I
want you to ask questions you're close as an oyster. There
on the porch your face looked like a little white mask. Inci-
dentally, did you know that your face is a triangle, with
the chin the apex? Rather a damaged chin at the moment!"

"And not as firm as I wish it were."

"It's your chin and you're stuck with it," Tay said un-gallantly. "But it's firm enough, a direct contradiction to that outsized, generous mouth of yours."

Karen sighed. "Oh, Tay, don't. Be unhappy if you want, that's why I'm walking with you. But don't try to talk telephone numbers."

"Be unhappy *your* way, you mean. God, how you like to label things! What would you do if you came across something you couldn't label? Oh, nothing as simple as my being in love with you or your being in love with me—" He stopped, said contritely, "I'm sorry. That was distinctly not Queensbury."

"It's all right." Her tone was weary.

"No, it's not all right but I've said it. I won't talk about that now. What would you do with an emotion you couldn't label, Karen?"

There was a little silence, only the soft pad-pad of their rubber-soled boots along the portage. "I would still try to label it," Karen said finally. "I would still want to stand back and look at it."

"Can you stand back and look at something that's an integral part of you?"

"You, a doctor, ask that?"

His quick answer was sarcastic. "Oh, now we have the 'physician, heal thyself' business."

Karen repeated steadily as though he had not spoken, "I would still want to stand back and look at it. And it can be labeled. It is hate, isn't it, Tay?"

"Yes."

"Hate tied up with something else, I think." Her breath

caught, strangled in her throat. "I said I wanted to help
if I could, but that I didn't want to ask questions. Tay,
it's impossible for me to ask questions under these circumstances. Any woman is a credulous fool who listens only to
the man's side of a—sex question."

Tay said with ironic admiration, "Well, well, the little
girl has been around. What are you afraid of, some more
of this misunderstood-husband whining?" Then he
stopped short, his hand left hers and gripped her elbow,
halting her also. "Karen, do you think that back of this
is just the usual marital mess?"

In the darkness Karen's voice was uncertain now for the
first time, a little weight of melancholy lifted from it.
"Naturally, that's what I thought."

He shook her. "It isn't true. Forget all that flubdub.
It isn't true. What is between Iris and me is something
that might just as well be between two men. A matter of
what she is, what she's done, quite aside from her having
married me. In short, as you've said, a matter of hate."

"Yet you married her in spite of it."

"I married her *because* of it."

Karen sighed again. "You see, I'm not the one for you
to talk to. You feel you can't tell me everything, so perhaps you should tell me nothing."

His laugh was despairing in the darkness. "I know."

Karen's hand suddenly closed over his. "Tay, if it were
just hate, good clean hate! You were never a sadist." Her
voice stumbled. "I was just a child when you were growing up, when you were a young man, and ten years difference was a big one then. But I remember you were always
so sharp, so definite about everything. You weren't ex-

ceptionally kind, at least in those soft, imaginative ways
that women notice, as Greg is. Without being effeminate,
he's the kindest person I've ever known."

Tay interrupted consideringly, wonderingly, "Yes, he
is."

"But your mind didn't work that way. Yet you were
always just, Tay, we could always count on that. And you
always seemed to sense when it was time to help. Even
when you were being lofty and single-track-minded, you
came down to earth when you were needed. I remember
that time when the truck broke down and we had to walk
those long miles up the portage. You were impatient because our legs weren't as long as yours, because we had to
plod along so slowly. And finally you strode ahead of us.
But then, Tay, you did come back, when it was getting
dark and my eight-year-old legs were beginning to wob-
ble. You came back and carried me that last half-mile to
the Lodge, grumbling and muttering all the time about
being saddled with kids. But you carried me." She hesitated, blurted suddenly, "There was never any cruelty in
you then."

"You mean I'm enjoying my hate."

"Yes, enjoying it for some dreadful reason that isn't you,
that can't be part of you."

"There was a doctor once that had to do a thing he
didn't want to do," he said abruptly, "something that was
against his every instinct as a man and a physician."

"Did he really *have* to do it? There was no alternative?"

"The alternative was even worse."

"Then I should think," Karen said carefully, "that he
actually *was* following his instincts as a man and a physi-

cian, even if in a way he hadn't expected." Her hand
pulled from his, folded pleadingly about his arm. "Tay,
I've been listening, listening so hard, but the words are a
jumble. It's as though you were talking to me in code. It
doesn't mean anything to me."

"Rain. East wind, rain," he said irrelevantly. He lifted
up his face, drank in the moisture-laden air. "Listen.
Can't you hear it back in the hills?" She stood obediently
still, hearing the wind rush across the treetops.

"Not with the moon still shining," she doubted. "But
it may pour before morning." They had come out into a
little open clearing, a knoll where the trees had reluctantly retreated and left a small meadow to clustering
partridge berry. The moon was higher now, smaller. Its
light was no longer a glory but a dimming lantern. Yet
after the Stygian darkness they had left, it seemed that by
this sudden light they could scrutinize each other's every
feature. And they did so, hungrily, gravely, facing each
other. Then by mutual consent they sat down on the log
near by; the "halfway log," it had always been called, for
it marked that distance from Lodge to beaver dam. Two
generations of feet had hollowed the earth immediately in
front of it, and now their own boots fitted into that hollow
familiarly, unconsciously.

Karen sat there silently for a moment. She had thrown
her head back and the soft dark curls lifted and settled and
lifted again under the fingers of the breeze. Her profile
was silhouetted clean-cut against the darkness of the tree
copse beyond her. The man stared at that profile, falling
silent himself. Finally she turned. "Tay, did you ever read
one of those silly old Victorian novels where someone

slipped an important letter under a door? And the right person didn't find it and everybody lived unhappily ever after—or at least until they were so old and gray nobody cared, least of all, the reader!"

"Yes, I remember." She sensed the smile in his voice and was encouraged.

"Well, I'm feeling just that way now, as though there were a letter I haven't found. Yet the essential thing has been said, that you don't—care for your wife. And if that's been said, then why—"

He said strongly, "That was not the only essential thing I said. I spoke of you and me."

"You've implied either too much or too little, I think, both about Iris and me. Is there any good reason, any real reason, why you can't be frank with me?"

He took her hand, held it closely. "There is something I believe about Iris, that I know about her—but that I still have to prove. Maybe I shall never be able to prove it. But in any case you must never be part of it, in any way. It must never touch you."

Her voice was very gentle. "But it has already touched me."

"No," he said, "no. Only my love has touched you. You haven't any part in what's between Iris and me. And in the years ahead I want you to remember that, to be able to remember it and be glad that it was like that." Suddenly he laughed. The sound held no humor. "I'm a hypocritical fool! I know it and you're thinking it. I have made you part of the picture, by everything I've said in the last hour I've made you part of it. But at least your part is involuntary, it needn't be more than that. You can forget what's been said tonight, what you saw in Iris' face, in my face this evening."

"If it's a question of helping you, I'd much rather take a voluntary part." Karen's voice was a whisper. "I don't want to be shut out if there's anything I can do to help you, Tay."

He turned and took her into his arms then, and for an instant she could see the reckless flash of his eyes in the moonlight, the jutting prow of his hard jawline. Then her own face was in merciful obscurity, pressed against his shoulder. "I'm in love with you, Karen, and that's the only way you can help. Love me and don't ask questions. Right at the start you said you wouldn't, and I'm going to hold you to it. For a time there I wanted you to ask. But that was only brutal, it could only hurt you without helping me." He repeated again, "This is the way you can help me. Let me hold you quietly. Like this." But his voice was despairing and the tension of his arms had no quietness.

The moon faded, receded behind a thickening curtain of mist. A partridge that had huddled motionless in a pine near by, winged across the glade now with sudden hardihood; and by the hidden, sunken brook twenty yards away, a fox moved again, his paws punctuating the mud with light neat asterisks as he followed the flight of the partridge.

"We should go back to the Lodge," Karen murmured. "No, Tay, no." She added dreamily, "Not that I care." Meaning to say I do care but this was all decided a million years ago and who am I to thrust my hands against you, even my highly evolved sentient intelligent hands? Her

words had no meaning to the man. But the sudden relaxed curve of her waist had meaning, that final arch of
the waist inclining in immemorial melancholy to the peremptory male arm. No longer merely supple. Suppliant.

He released her, stood up, brushed a hand across his
forehead, his eyes. "Yes," he said heavily, "we should go
back. Now."

They talked little as they walked back; and then only of
the small immediacies of the night, the plank on the
bridge that should be fastened and whether the rustle far
back in the woods were deer or fox. But near the guides'
cabin, Tay halted her.

"Karen," he said hesitantly, "I'm not sure, I can't be
sure, but I think the venom is gone. Perhaps I can thank
you for that."

Karen said quietly, "Only for speaking of it, Tay. There
in the living room tonight you reached the peak of that
feeling—and it struck her down." She drew a long breath.
"Another step and it could strike you down."

"Afraid for my sanity?" But his tone wasn't amused.

She caught at his hand. "No, for your quality, Tay.
For your personality, the rightness you've always had."

He said slowly, "I said the venom was gone. I didn't
say the hate was gone."

She tried to laugh. "Maybe Webster wouldn't say so,
but I like the distinction. Venom spreads inward too
much."

He said again with persistent emphasis, "But you're not
afraid for my sanity?"

"Good heavens, no!" Her voice was really merry now.
"It's not like you to keep harping on that."

His own voice was lighter too. "Good. Remember that, it might prove important sometime. I'm a careful man in the woods, my pet, and I don't have morose 'accidents' with guns. Never let anyone sell you that idea."

Karen's hands grew very cold. "Tay, are you trying to tell me—?"

He tucked her arm in his and turned her steps toward the Lodge. "Not trying to tell you a thing except that I have a lot to live for, I've discovered tonight," he said cheerfully, "and you are to squawk to high heaven if I'm not given that chance. Now hop to bed. I'm going to have another pipe before I turn in."

At the steps he released her arm casually; and Karen understood with mixed disappointment and approval that those moments back on the portage would not be repeated, not until many circumstances were changed. Now he must stride ahead as he had done when she was very young. She must watch him go from her and be left to wonder what dark unblazed terrain he walked; left to wonder whether this time, when he wished to retrace his steps to her, the decision would be entirely his. Her knees were even weaker now than they had been that time long years ago when she had stumbled hopelessly, stubbornly along in the darkness, her eight-year-old eyes longing only for the lights of the Lodge; her only comfort, Gregory's quiet little voice at her side.

"And if you get *too* tired," he had reassured her stoutly, "we can just bunk down in the meadow until someone comes after us. I will take care of you." But then Tay had come back. And in the rush of that relief, in the utter weariness that struck her as Tay boosted her to his shoulder, she had forgotten to answer Gregory. A little smile twisted Karen's lips. I will thank Greg tomorrow, she thought, and he will laugh and try to remember.

She undressed in the darkness and was just slipping into bed when a flashlight glowed from the other side of the room. Iris was turning the light on her wrist watch.

"Are you feeling better?" Karen asked calmly.

"Yes. Nice walk?"

"Fine. Good night."

"Good night. I don't need to wish you happy dreams," Iris said deliberately. There was a click and the room was in darkness again.

IT WAS EARLY, so early that the guides' cabin was still dark. And no one's plans for the day involved starting out before breakfast. Even after Iris' collapse had proved only a mild indigestion, it had been tacitly assumed that for her sake the household should not be astir too early. But Gregory had been awake nearly all night. Toward dawn he had dozed and wakened from that doze alert, though he lay quietly for a time. The other men were still deep in sleep except for one truculent snore from Tay, as though his dreams were uneasy. That sound was cut short by the sleeper himself. Gregory smiled in the darkness. In concentration camp Tay's subconscious must have learned the art of sleeping inconspicuously. In fact, Tay claimed that he had once done a two hours' march sound asleep. Gregory rather doubted that.

He slipped out of bed, adjusted the awkward brace on his leg and, gathering his clothes together, started to tiptoe from the room. His father stirred and sighed and said very quietly, "Greg?"

Gregory moved to his side and pressed an admonitory hand on his father's shoulder. "Everyone's asleep, Dad. Don't wake 'em."

"Good hunting, son." His father smiled with one drowsy eye, then huddled under the covers again.

The Judge had forgotten. Greg wasn't going hunting; he was going on the river as he had announced the night

before. The fire in the great black stove had died during
the night and he dressed rapidly, shivering into three pair
of socks as well as other extra clothing. But the pleasantly
quiet mood in which he had waked still held him. Under
his breath he even hummed with a little grin, " 'Why
should I wait and watch tonight, when all the Lodge is
still?' " That reminded him, the old portable gramophone
and ancient records were still down in the boathouse. The
family were all thoroughly tired of *The Lover's Flute* and
The William Tell Overture and *The Land of the Sky-
Blue Water* and a host of other thin and scratchy records.
But ever since an armful of disks had crashed on the bluff,
Karen had established a firm law against taking new records to the boathouse. There was no law, however, against
stealing new needles. Gregory pocketed a couple, against
the chance that the salmon too would be sleepy this early,
and that his foray might develop merely into a dozing
hour in the old dugout.

He selected his rod and stepped out on the terrace. Behind him the forests were dark and the river was still invisible under a hundred-foot blanket of mist. But as he
trudged along the portage, the filaments of his flashlight
became a red skeleton under the pearly light from the east,
and presently he pocketed the torch. Gregory had walked
this road since he was old enough to toddle but he never
tired of it. From hour to hour and season to season the
woods and rivers and mountains across the river varied.
And the portage itself, under the snows and rains that
swept it, produced new brooks or upthrust an unsuspected
boulder.

He came to the open space now, where the dawn had

blown away the mist. The rough little meadow was covered with a thick scalp of the low red partridge berry and
here an odd phenomenon had taken place. Thick cob-
webs on the bushes had caught the mist that elsewhere had
dissipated, so that serried rows of fluffy white balls dotted
the meadow symmetrically. Here in New Brunswick, in
an October dawn, was the mirage of a southern cotton
field. Even as Gregory looked, a ray from the still unseen
sun struck from far down the river, fingered through the
red of the bushes so that for an instant a low flame, frothed
with white, burned across the field. Then flame and cotton bolls alike disappeared. Gregory sighed contentedly.
"The fiery bush," he smiled to himself. The portage had
never yet disappointed him and it seemed that this morning it was giving an extra fine show. That meant luck on
the river too, perhaps. It was not, after all, going to rain,
not for a few hours anyway.

He glanced at the halfway log and noted the fresh foot-
prints that lay in front of it. Two people had sat here
only a few hours before. This was where Tay and Karen
had been then, during those long hours when he had lain
awake and wondered. His forehead drew into a little
frown, then smoothed quickly. Why shouldn't they walk
together, two old friends? As restless and wakeful as he
had been no doubt, under the disturbance Iris' illness had
caused.

A quarter of a mile farther along, where the bluff sloped
more easily, he struck through the thinning woods to the
river. This route, which only he had the necessity to use,
swung past the site of an old French-Indian skirmish.
Neither tourist nor historian had ever passed this way.

Gregory paused thoughtfully by a tree which still held a half-embedded bullet. Almost it seemed sacrilegious, but he worked away at it with his knife until the leaden slug fell into his palm. Iris might be interested, though he dropped the bullet into his pocket doubtfully. There were enormous lacunae in her knowledge of her continent's history; and at that, this bullet might seem dull indeed to someone who had lived in Asia, where civilization was recorded in the thousands, rather than the hundreds, of years.

Once at the shore he climbed into the dugout, poled it slowly upriver toward the old boathouse. The curtain of mist had lifted high now, but the river still ran black and silent. He pulled in toward the boathouse and sat there glancing up at the almost sheer cliff. Farther to his left and almost at the bend, the shreds of the old steps still clung. The Lodge, of course, was invisible, closed off by the height of the bluff. He wondered if Iris were awake yet and what her waking would be: blank and sagging as her face had looked when he left her, or languid and sure again? Gregory thought: I am glad that her illness didn't mean what I guessed at first, but it isn't a gladness for myself. Those two shouldn't have children. They dislike each other.

He knew now that he had sensed that latter fact since the first night on the train. He sighed, suddenly disinclined for the rod after all. But the trend his thoughts were taking had become lax, self-indulgent. With determination he struggled into his hip-length river boots and climbed from the dugout. He stepped into the stream and pulled the boat to the bank. He couldn't go too far from the shore with no guide to assist should he take an unwary step and his bad foot betray him. But he could at least stand out a little into the river and strip his mind of every-thing but the morning and the salmon rod. And because it was a schooled mind, it obeyed.

A warmth came into the air, the mist was almost gone and presently, although the sun was still low, the surface of the water began to come alive with small diamonds. The scent of birch and pine grew stronger and the far reaches of the river began to uncoil to his eyes in a heavenly stretch of blue and green ripple, flecked with myriad circles where each rock flung out its own small whirlpool. The woods, their predominant green threaded with the gold and scarlet of the deciduous trees, were still wrapped in sleep, cupping between their emerald palms the morning liveliness of the water, hushing it to a sedate murmur.

Gregory threw back his head, drinking in the tart north air. This moment was good, and he had learned long ago the hard sure lesson of living in and by these small mo-ments. If one tasted them to the full, they were not so small after all, he reflected, and in the aggregate they often proved a formidable bulwark against—well, against the mo-ments that were not so good. Whatever came, one accepted it, not breaking; bending as the supple rod must bend to the water after its high skyward flash. But a morning and a moment like this were not merely to be accepted; they were to be accepted with reverence; the feel of the rod in his hands, the slap of the water against his rubber-clad thighs, the air, the woods, the river. Above all, the silence and the solitariness that were not loneliness. For a time he could enjoy the conceit that a new day was being minted for him alone, a gold coin about to be spun to him from that far river stretch where the sun had just burst fully.

He knew suddenly that he was happy, with a serenity that had no root in mental process. And he thought with a slow, amused wonderment: Underneath the pain I have always been happy. Always. So perhaps I'm essentially mindless. His smile deepened. He stood very still, the rod quiet in his hands. The small pebbles tugged and shifted beneath his feet and the current complained, but he was braced against them.

Presently he began to move slowly upriver, toward the sun.

It was to be a day of small things, apparently. The first mail in ten days had come in, brought by the truck that carried fresh provisions. Judge Littlefield and Iris sat alone over the scattered letters and papers, their coffee cups pushed aside. There had been only one letter for Iris and she had scanned that rapidly, thrown it down. "The house will be a mess," she said.

"Trouble?" The Judge looked up mildly from his own mail.

"A note from Ester, thanking me for giving them all a vacation while we're away!"

"And didn't you?"

"Certainly I didn't! The attics needed a thorough cleaning out—all that junk of Tay's from the warehouse—and there were other things too. As it was, they had plenty of leisure on their hands, with the family away. But they've closed the house and skipped, if you please, until two days before we go home!"

The Judge was still mild. "That's a bit unusual, without permission," he agreed.

"Oh, they had permission." If Iris ever flushed, her color would have been high. As it was, only her thinned lips carried her irritation. "Tay wired them from Fredericton that they might as well take a complete vacation if they wanted. And they did want, of course. I do think he might have consulted me."

Judge Littlefield smiled, shook his head. "The average male thinks that housework consists solely of two things, dishes and beds," he admitted. "But America isn't Asia. During the war we learned to be very tender with our domestic staffs. I suppose Tay thought it was an excellent time to be generous. He should have consulted you but don't worry. From what I've seen of Ester, everything will be in apple-pie order when you return."

Iris' frown smoothed a little. "She is competent," she acknowledged. But her annoyance still lingered. Under the prod of it she said with an ungraciousness that was not typical in her dealings with him, "I don't need anyone to stay with me. Why aren't you hunting, as you planned?"

"Oh, I'm going out soon but I was lazy. Karen and Tay got away late too. Greg was the only early bird."

Iris picked up a newspaper. "Karen and Tay hunting together?" she asked casually. The Judge strolled over and glanced at the slate to see if any corrections had been made since the night before. "No, she's taken off from Bear Trap and he's working west from Springy Landing. They're not within miles of each other. Everyone's alone today. The guides are taking the other side of the river, south and east. No deer yet—and time is running short."

"Springy Landing. That's where I left my scarf the other night when Greg and I walked down there." She picked up her paper again and he politely returned to his own mail. Her thoughts were not on the headlines, however. She had omitted to mention why the scarf had been forgotten. The scarf was long and wide and she had spread it on the bending grasses that furred the shore, and had invited Greg to sit there beside her.

"More comfortable than that log, Greg."

"Thanks, but I'd need a derrick to lift me up afterward. This foot is no good as a lever."

"I'll help you. Sit here with me and watch the moon."

He had finally lowered himself to the ground beside her. Sitting there they could peer through the long grasses at the rising moon. It had been a little like the jungle and some of the jungle excitement had stirred in her. The moonlight had struck across Greg's pale hair, his broad shoulders and his square face that was so young in its contours, so pain-quieted around the eyes. Half-recumbent as he had been then, as he had been forced to be because of the leg stretched before him, she had been able to forget for a moment that handicap of his that so irked her. There was virility in him and some other force, a force that she wanted to tear from its insulation and touch with intimate hands.

They had talked desultorily for a time and then, almost imperceptibly, she had settled back against his shoulder. "It's so comfortable being with you, Greg. Like coming home." Her tone was drowsy with invitation. She felt his shoulder tense against her, heard him swallow.

But after a long moment he had only said, "Be at home, Iris. With all of us." It wasn't the right answer. She had cast about, trying again. And this time her face had turned to his, very close to his so that the perfume of her hair was on his cheek.

"With all of you? I feel so lost, Greg, sometimes. Let me into your own world once in a while, will you? Tay shuts me out of his." That had been fatal, mentioning Tay's name. She should have known it, she had thought with instant vexation. For Greg had closed his eyes, as though making a last relinquishment of the perfume and nearness of her.

"I can't imagine Tay's doing that." Then, pleasantly, "It's growing chilly, don't you think? We'd better walk back or I'll be blamed for letting you catch cold." He hadn't waited for her answer. With a thrust of those muscular arms of his he had started to scramble up, somehow, from the ground. On one knee, he had paused a moment, waiting perhaps for the hand she had promised a few moments before. But though she had quickly sprung to her feet, her arms remained folded; so that Gregory was forced to drag himself erect with ludicrous awkwardness.

She had not even turned her eyes away, she had watched. Yes, there was force in him, she still acknowledged coolly. Then let it stand back and look at itself now, posturing, if only briefly, as a clumsy four-legged animal. Yet Greg's voice had been casual enough as they had turned back toward the portage. It had held its usual friendliness and quietness, with no hint of injured male pride. She shrugged inwardly: He was, then, inured to these small physical humiliations; they had become part of him. Her original distaste which had been buried for weeks under the flattery of his admiration, flowered now into full contempt. His admiration was sterile for he had rejected her overtures.

Her voice had been more softly kind than ever as they had walked back to the Lodge, for it lay on the muffling velvet of her malice.

"Your scarf," the Judge was saying, "is over there, on the mantel." She glanced up, startled from her trivial reminiscence, startled by the laugh in his voice. She stared at him a moment suspiciously, almost ready to believe that he had read her thoughts or that Gregory had made some careless comment about that half-hour at Springy Landing. But the Judge went on merrily:

"I picked it up from the Landing on my way home yesterday, and had a little fun with Ben about it. He's been looking for that porcupine that's been hanging around the guides' cabin. He joined me on the portage and asked where I had found the scarf. So I told him that I had seen his porcupine strolling along the portage early yesterday —and added that the porcupine had your scarf neatly wound around its neck. It was a cold morning, you remember. Well, Ben opened and shut his mouth like a dying fish. Then he just shook his head and said: 'Judge, you been around me too much!' "

Iris smiled vaguely. "Did he get the porcupine?"

"No, but I saw it just a while ago, near the portage." The Judge yawned and selected a gun from the rack.

"There's a bounty on the nose, and I suppose Ben could use the money."

"Oh, it's waiting around to be shot?" Iris asked with sarcasm.

"Sometimes it seems like that, and I wager I'll find him. Come along?"

"I may as well." It would be pleasant to find the Judge fallible.

But the porcupine was still there. After walking a few hundred yards down the portage they saw it, hunched in a small pine that jutted from the bluff's edge. As they approached, the animal froze to the tree. It was very near, near enough.

"Let me try a shot," Iris said suddenly. The Judge relinquished the gun with a little air of surprise. Though Iris had a hunting permit, this was the first time he had seen her interested in anything more than target shooting, at which she was still very inept. As she raised the gun, the porcupine's curiosity overcame its timidity. It peered around a branch of the pine, its small black-gloved hands resting confidently on the trunk. Above the round snub nose its eyes studied them inquisitively.

Iris fired. The animal flinched, the ridiculous little hands began slipping, scrabbling along the tree trunk. She fired again but the porcupine still clung to its perch. As she raised the gun a third time, she felt Judge Littlefield take it from her hands. There was a sharp retort as he pressed the trigger. The animal fell cleanly, the crash of its fall echoing down the bluff. "Sorry," Judge Littlefield said dryly, "but it was wounded. Better to finish it off quickly."

Iris covered her eyes for an instant with a quick, femi-
nine gesture. "Ugh! He looked so human I could hardly
hold the gun steady. Those comical little paws! How do
you ever have the courage to kill them anyway!"

"Because they're pests, and do more damage around a
camp than rats." He added with rebuking emphasis, "But
it's better not to handle a gun at all if you can't give the
coup de grâce."

She looked up at him admiringly. "I do hope some day
I can learn to be properly cold-blooded." His frown
smoothed at that and he laughed.

"Properly cold-blooded and swiftly merciful," he
amended. He marked a tree to guide Ben to the spot
where the porcupine lay, and they returned to the Lodge.
As he replaced the emptied weapon and selected a heavier
gun, he looked inquiringly at Iris. "Sure you won't be
lonesome? No one will be back for lunch. Well, Gregory
perhaps, if he's had luck."

"I'm never lonesome," Iris said promptly. Because of
that silly porcupine he had been a little displeased with
her, she knew, and now graciousness rather than further
petulance seemed advisable. "Do run along. Here I have
a feast of new magazines, not to mention the fact that I
haven't seen a newspaper for days."

"If you feel the urge to walk any of the trails, take a look
at the slate first," he warned and she nodded again.

With his going the day grew suddenly colder. The sun
was higher in the sky now but it held no warmth, only a
light that mocked her dark mood. Since she had waked
this morning, Iris had firmly fended away the thought of
the night before, of Tay's eyes, of all that the revelation

must mean between them and to the shadow of the relationship to which they still pretended. He would not
be able to pretend much longer, even in front of others.
That much was clear. But whether in their first moment
alone he would throw the gauntlet down openly, she did
not know. Nor did she intend to be alone with him until
she could plan a counterattack or defense.

Right now she couldn't seem to think clearly. A curious
lassitude, born either of the shock of the night before or
of her uneasy, drugged sleep, still held her. Could she
make some deal with Tay—a divorce, perhaps? He was
obviously in love with Karen, even if he didn't know it yet.
Iris' fingers drummed nervously on the table. She might
be able to work that, for Tay still had no proof, no proof
at all. It was still his word against hers, his wild speculation against her alibis. Even her faint of the night before
had meant nothing except to Tay. She was thankful for
these intervening hours, for Greg's medicine. If Tay had
accused her in concrete terms last night she might have
broken—finally. Now she was strong again, or stronger at
least. She would deny everything, admit nothing. Against
that he was helpless, doll or no doll. At thought of the
doll, that curious weakness flooded her wrists again . . .

She shook herself impatiently, opened a magazine,
pushed it aside; glanced at a headline, her eyes unseeing.
A gaudy Sunday supplement, its cover featuring a black-
haired, slant-eyed beauty, was also about to be discarded.
Then suddenly her eyes saw, widened, her hands bracketed
the paper to the table because they could not hold the
pages up.

YOKOHAMA LILY IN AMERICA?

The caption inquired in scarlet, writhing letters.

The room whirled, then quieted again. Iris reached across the table unsteadily, took from her knitting bag the spectacles that were still a secret to everyone else, and adjusted them. She forced herself to light a cigarette, to relight it when her first spent breath blew out the match. And now she would read the article, calmly, coldly. This meant nothing either; similar headlines had, at intervals, met her eyes before; in Cairo, in Lisbon, elsewhere. She had sipped a cognac over one of them and had felt an indifferent amusement. She could feel an indifferent amusement now if she tried. But that was before Tay . . .

The article was, after all, the same old rehash of speculations and absurdities, sprinkled with vague references to Messalinas and Borgias; as though, she thought contemptuously, every feature writer were suckled on the same two pages of history and those alone. Only toward the end of the article was there anything new.

The song "Home, Sweet Home" with which the Lily signed off, is also her unique signature, for records of her broadcasts show that she sang a certain musical phrase in the song incorrectly each time. Whether this was intentional or not, we can't know. But we can be grateful in either case, for the song that millions of Americans know and love still remains our song. Lily never sang it as the humblest mothers and the greatest prima donnas have sung it. Never. Through some strange twist of her mind or some even stranger twist of Providence, she never sang "Home, Sweet Home" as we know it. The song remains ours, to be sung as true Americans have always sung it.

And who knows? At this very moment, in some gay night

club or some dark waterfront café, Yokohama Lily may be singing her signature again, unwittingly signing her own death warrant!

Iris stared unseeingly down at the blotchy marginal sketch of a gray-haired mother nursing an unbelievably young infant, and at an even blotchier drawing presumably indicating Jenny Lind, judging by the hoop skirts.

"What phrase—*what* phrase did I sing wrong?" she whispered aloud and then clapped a hand to her mouth. The cigarette dropped to the floor and she stepped on it automatically. What phrase? She looked wildly around and then slumped back in her chair. No, of course there wouldn't be a songbook here in the wilderness where only the radio and victrola offered music. A signature, a damning signature! *That* was what Tay had been waiting for—and had never secured.

But Gregory had! And behind Greg she could see a wall becoming transparent and behind that wall a machine and a disk whirling. A disk whirling away her life. Damn Greg, damn him.

She stood up, paced the room, tried to order her thinking. Tay couldn't know—yet. He couldn't possibly know. Here were the days of the calendar, staring at her smirkingly from the wall. On this afternoon, late, she had sung for Greg. Tay and Karen had come in; Greg and Karen had left later. Iris hadn't dressed for dinner that night, she had been with Tay every minute. And he had left almost immediately after dinner and had taxied to Boston. He had been in Boston that night and the next day and the next night, except for a brief hour when he had hur-

ried out to the house to inspect his gear; and again to go
with her to the station. He had no opportunity—she was
sure he had had no opportunity to go into the music room,
to get at that hidden secret space. Nor did he have any
reason to think there had been any necessity for it. He
couldn't know she had sung for Greg, nor what she had
sung. Again it was obvious even to Iris' frantic mind that
Tay did not know—yet. She wouldn't be here if he had
that proof for which he had been working and waiting
with such deadly patience.

Rare tears flooded her eyes. If only her father were here
or Fritz were here! Or even Marie. It was terrible and
desolating that she should have to face this alone, all alone.
She took off her glasses, stared at their misted lenses.
When had she cried before, cried like this? She couldn't
remember. She wiped her eyes, laid the glasses on the
table and drew a long determined breath.

Well, she *was* alone, and she had been in tighter spots
than this. It was simply that her courage had grown
weaker; it had been thinned, diluted by these long weeks
of spineless peace and routine and surface friendliness.
She drew a tumbler of water from the faucet in the hall
that was fed by the icy spring far down the portage. She
was calmer. And now, finally, she was calm. She held up
a hand, studied it. It had ceased trembling. The weakness
had vanished, the fainting terror.

An electric potency flooded her as though every gland
were pouring forth power, every nerve stripping itself for
some final victorious test.

There were two immediate things: the record of her
song that day in the "control room." And secondly,

Gregory; Gregory who at any moment might drop some careless remark about her singing that particular song. She would make him promise that he would never mention that she had sung it. He would promise, she knew, whatever wild tale she spun for him as an excuse. And he would keep that promise—until or unless he saw some article such as this one; or until Tay, perhaps, spoke openly of his suspicions. And after last night, she could not know what Tay might do, what he might say.

Iris lifted the top of the stove and crammed the supplement into the embers. It was only a brief respite, she knew. Tomorrow or next week or next month there would be a similar reference and Gregory would see it. Or Tay, despairing of ever springing his trap, would speak of the song to Gregory. A wax record could be destroyed, it was inanimate. But Gregory . . .

Her mind hovered a moment over the image of Gregory, drifted back to the wax record. It wouldn't be simple, but somehow, in some way, she must reach the house before Tay did, must enter that secret room and destroy the disk. Or destroy Tay first. She pulled at her lower lip thoughtfully. That latter course would be the most desirable of all, as things stood now. But it would be the most difficult and dangerous to accomplish. Had he, for instance, left any written statement, perhaps with his lawyer, that would point a direct finger at her in case of any unfortunate accident? She doubted it. He was too sure of his own wariness, his own shrewdness. He would keep this his own game too, until the last possible moment. And then pounce. That is what she thought, but she couldn't be sure of it. It was a terrible chance on which to gamble.

Tay was no longer a challenging excitement in her blood, a heady stimulant to her voracious appetite for power. He was stark danger. Last night the danger had crouched. But now with the sound of a disk, with even the briefest testimony from Gregory, it could spring.

Tay, Gregory, a record. Two of these three must be smashed. There was no other course, no other possible road.

Iris went to her room and changed from her lounging robe into her tweeds and walking boots. In the living room again, she paused by the slate where Tay's writing scrawled boldly: "West and north from Springy Landing." On second thought she returned to her room and pulled on a soft, scarlet beret. It wouldn't be pleasant to be mistaken for a deer. Money: she took her own small purse and in the men's dormitory found Tay's wallet, which she denuded. She was walking steadily, purposefully as she pulled on her gloves and went to the gun rack. Anyone watching her as she stepped out on the porch would have noted with what practiced familiarity this woman carried the weapon, a woman who a short time before had been unable to hit a porcupine squarely from a distance of twenty-five feet. But no one was watching.

Iris hadn't walked far along the portage when the thin yet definite sound came to her ears, and for a moment struck her motionless. Music, coming from the river. The day was still young, the sun still climbing higher; but her immersion in the darkness of her thoughts had been so complete, her sense of physical isolation so strong, that the strains of the gramophone seemed a jeering anachronism. She didn't hesitate long, but threading her way through the underbrush reached the edge of the bluff. She laid the gun aside and lowering herself to the ground, cautiously peered through the bushes.

Gregory was seated on the bank, was wrestling himself valiantly out of one of his river boots. The dugout was drawn to the shore, but one end rocked gently in the stream; and within the boat she could see the silver gleam that indicated he had had some luck with salmon. Propped on the bench beside Gregory, the gramophone screechingly asserted again that a policeman's life is not a n'appy one. The words were not clear from this distance, and for that matter the record had long ago given up any attempt at diction. But Iris remembered the song, though she had only heard it once. Too bad, she thought grimly and bitterly, that Jules' ears had not been equally good. That day when he had taught her an incorrect phrase, he had laid the fuse that was now perilously consuming her remaining time. One doesn't argue with a fuse. One stamps it out. At Jules' door, then, could be laid whatever steps she might have to take, now or in the future.

The river was clear, so clear.

In one breathless, audacious flash, her course was equally clear. And she was well out of hearing of the Lodge. Yet still she waited and as she waited the music stopped. She glanced down again. Gregory had paused, one boot thrown aside. He was reaching over, was replacing one record with another, was winding the ancient mechanism again.

"Greg!" she called. "Greg!"

He glanced up and his hand dropped from the needle's

arm. He clambered to his feet and called back gaily,
"Iris?"

"Greg, Karen has been seriously hurt! Come at once!"

His voice was controlled. "What happened?" After a
moment, forcibly, "Is she dead?" The words came to her
attenuated, but as distinct as though he had been standing
eight feet away, instead of more than eighty feet below her.

"No, gun accident! All the men are gone. She needs
you—now! Can you climb up here? I don't mean where
the steps were—that's impossible, I know—but here. The
guides have done it. You haven't time to go clear way
around. It would take forty minutes at least."

"Yes." She saw his shoulders square themselves; knew,
though she could not see, that his eyes were rapidly travel-
ing the face of the bluff. She watched him with a heady
excitement that was almost physical pain. In such a moment as this, it seemed that she had always been able to
ride, almost literally, another's mind; that she could feel
herself whipped and tossed with that mind as it cast frantically here and there. And she could ride such a vehicle
with exhilaration, knowing that it was no more an integral
part of her than is a careening roller coaster an integral
part of its passenger. Less so, in fact, for one could detach
oneself from a mind even while it was in midflight . . .

Gregory was not really conscious of thinking as he surveyed the bluff. But his subconscious had firmly put Karen
herself aside for the immediate problem. It had been years
since he had made this ascent. But he saw that the small
tree still held at a certain point; that at another point the
outcropping of rock was still uneroded. The stretch of
pine needle could still be negotiated as it had always been,

by frank use of shoulder, hip and heel. There remained
—he drew a long breath—there remained that last impossible eight feet. Impossible, because it demanded the unerring use of the one foot and leg which were now in-
capacitated. His determination would need a miracle.

And the miracle happened. It literally unfolded.

From the top of the cliff he saw the multicolored scarf
drop the folds of its seven-foot length: Iris' scarf, that had
once been an Indian cashmere shawl. Iris' shawl, that had
once been a seat in the moonlight grasses. She had forgotten the proffered hand that time, and now the scarf was
coming to make amends. It was almost as though Iris, bless
her, had been inside his mind; as though her keen eyes
had seen at once every hazard of the cliff that it had taken
him years to learn as a youngster. He shrugged aside the
thought of the one rubber boot he was wearing, its sole
worn smooth. It wouldn't have the grip his wood boots
afforded, but he didn't dare take the time to change. It
would be too long a task with the impeding brace. And
fortunately his good foot was stockinged, not booted.

Iris watched, her heart pounding. It was, she thought,
like watching a great blond ape moving along the face of
a precipice. For Gregory's arms again and again performed
not only their allotted responsibilities but that of his
maimed foot as well. Presently she saw him throw himself
on his back, where the rock became a pine needle carpet;
or rather, not a carpet but a tapestry, for it hung almost
vertically. He inched himself along it, his shoulders digging in, his fingers literally boring grips in the earth, his
hips wedging themselves into invisible hollows. Now he had
righted himself, had turned, had found a handhold. In

another moment he would be able to, he would, in fact, have to, clutch at the scarf.

Iris herself lay face downward, her feet hooked around a small bush, her hands clenched on two corners of the scarf; clenched so hard that the knuckles stood out small and blue. Only her face projected over the cliff edge, loose gold hair hanging free; her face, and the hands that held the scarf. He was very near her now, near enough so she could see the perspiration runnelling his cheeks.

"Are you braced?" he asked, and though his voice was jerky, it was still quiet.

"Yes."

"I'm going to grab the scarf and jump for that bush," he said. "You won't have to take the weight more than five seconds—three seconds. Just hang on those three seconds. That's all you have to do."

"Yes." She tried to add a reassuring word, could not.

Gregory half-rose, lunged at the scarf with one hand, grasped it. In the same instant his unmaimed foot gave a last thrust at the loose shale beneath it, his knee bent like a swimmer's as his free hand thrust out strongly and surely for the sustaining bush. It was a powerful, unerring assertion of shoulder, arms and nerve; his whole body ignoring the swinging useless leg. In that split second she knew he would succeed.

Iris' hands unclamped from the scarf.

She saw Gregory's eyes wide and astonished on hers as he hurtled backward; as one foot caught, bent, was freed; as he hurtled backward again. It was not a clean fall, sharp and sure. It was a gantlet of rock and ledge and pine

stump and ledge and stump and rock. While the vehicle
that was Gregory's mind still careened in midflight, Iris
quietly detached herself from it . . .

She sat back on the ground for a long time, absently examining her fingers. Two nails were broken. There had
been, as a matter of fact, almost a second when her hands
had willed to hold to the scarf against the orders of her
mind. Hence, the broken nails. But she mustn't sit here
staring. There was more to be done. For one thing, the
scarf must be retrieved. It had whipped and snapped and
coiled and unfolded like a flag as it had followed Gregory's
flight. It lay with him now, frozen to his hand.

Finally she rose to her feet, and still keeping concealed
behind the bushes, she stared up and down the river. It
was silent, untenanted. She picked up the gun and walked
back to the portage; walked up it until, though she still
could not see the Lodge, she could hear the faint sound of
the kitchen radio. Then she retraced her steps, continued
down the portage until the bluff became a comfortable
slope. She discarded the gun again and cautiously scrambled down toward the shore. It was no shore actually,
only a shore line defined in reedy grass and mud and rock,
so that the hem of her tweed suit was soaking and heavy
long before she came to where Gregory was lying. It didn't
matter. She wasn't really conscious of any discomfort.

He lay quite easily, half on his face as though he were
asleep. He was in almost the exact spot where she had
seen him first, for his discarded boot lay near by and the
gramophone was only a few feet away. She felt for the
pulse in his wrist, but now her hands became so suddenly

unsteady that she could not tell whether it was the throb
of her heart or his that she felt.

"Greg," she said, "it's Iris. Are you badly hurt?"

She couldn't be sure, but she thought his jacket moved
then, that he breathed, once and heavily. She looked
around, then down. A large jagged stone lay near his
head. She reached for it, paused without touching it. She
pulled on the gloves which she had removed when she had
gripped the scarf, and stumbled to her feet. She pressed
the lever of the gramophone, adjusted the needle. Some
sounds are easier to bear than others. Then she returned
to Gregory's side, crouched, reached for the stone again.

"Greg, dear," she said composedly, "it's Iris. Speak to
me. You're all right. Speak to me." She sat back on her
haunches, watched him steadily. He did not move, did
not murmur. But now she was sure that she had seen the
unconscious betraying movement of his breath. She looked
up and down the river. Her hand curled casually and
easily around the stone. Tightened. Her eyes saw the exact spot on his exposed right temple.

Gregory was not conscious. There were only dreams:
A vague uneasiness about Karen that faded away somehow
into his father's eyes looking over a blanket good hunting son and the voice of Iris very tender and the sky-blue
water and her heart is not afraid. And then the voices
were gone and the uneasiness, and he was walking up the
river toward the sun again.

With the brassy clang of cymbals, river and sky suddenly
smote each other. Gregory walked into the sun with a free
stride, without wonder and without pain.

"And I came to her Lodge at dawning," the gramophone

scratchily declared. The needle leaped a worn groove, went on doggedly: "She is sick for the Sky-Blue Water." It stuck, hesitated, repeated with a gentle and inane persistence: "Sky-Blue Water, Sky-Blue Water, Sky-Blue Water—" The record slowed to a complete stop.

As Iris came out on the portage again it began to rain. The sun had been dimming, clouding the last few minutes, but even in spite of that warning the rain came unexpectedly to her. The air had hesitated, promised the night before; but with the morning the sun had conquered. Now it suddenly gave up the unequal battle and the woods were athrum with the steady beat of the water. The ruts of the portage turned into miniature rivulets.

Iris stood undecided, glanced at her wrist watch. Though she had taken money with her against the possibility that she might not return to the Lodge, that original idea could be altered by the fact that she had met Gregory instead of Tay. And she was still near the Lodge. She knew the truck was due to return to the village as soon as the driver had had his lunch, an early one. She could ride back with him. In that case she might return to the Lodge, leave the gun, pick up some luggage and make a more formal departure for the benefit of the kitchen staff. She imagined that brief conversation with Mrs. Lawrence, the housekeeper.

"I'm still not feeling too well, Mrs. Lawrence, and I think I'll go to Fredericton and be comfortably ill in a hotel bed there, where it's warm. The others will be coming out in a week anyway, and I'll just wait there for them."

Of course she could imagine Mrs. Lawrence's protests,

her insistence that Iris should wait for her husband's return from the day's hunting; that the truck should wait
for that return. But she had an answer for that too.

"If I do, he'd insist on going with me. Perhaps all the
others would insist too. And it would be silly for them
to cut their vacation short just because I've had a little
digestive upset. They'd be nice about it but you know
they'd be disappointed, particularly since no one's had
any luck with deer yet." Mrs. Lawrence would still be
dubious and upset but she would be helpless. After all,
she was an employee, with no right to argue beyond a certain point. And Iris would be able to pack, to put on dry
clothes, to leave with some semblance of dignity. Every
move that could be interpreted reasonably, however im-
pulsive her actions might seem, would leave more roads
open. Too many had been closed to her already.

It was still all very reasonable, but now, shivering in the
increasing downpour, Iris was reluctant to go ahead with
that plan. What if one of the hunters, discouraged by the
rain, was on the way back, had already returned? Or what
if Mrs. Lawrence proved overconscientious, insisted on
journeying with Iris to Fredericton, waited to make sure
she was really not more ill than she professed? There were
too many ifs, particularly that dread one: What if by some
mischance she were forced to be present when Gregory's
body was discovered? At the moment she did not feel
equal to the further acting that situation would demand.

No, it was better to discard the whole idea and drive
ahead with the really urgent matter, getting back to Boston
with no possibility of interruption.

She turned and started walking down the portage resolutely. Ordinarily the truck wouldn't start for another half hour, at least; but it was possible, it was more than probable, that with this downpour it would start out immediately, the driver hoping to keep ahead of the bogs that even now must be forming. And presently above the sound of the rain that was now torrential, she heard without surprise the sound of the motor, felt the ground vibrate beneath her feet.

She stepped to one side of the portage and as soon as the truck had rumbled abreast of her, she stood out from the underbrush and waved it to a halt. Lanny Thompson, the driver, stared at her with a mild wonderment.

"Better git back to the Lodge, Mrs. Harrison," he called above the throb of the motor and the rain, "Mrs. Lawrence is raising Cain about you being out in the wet after you was sick last night."

Iris thrust the gun under the tarpaulin that covered the tonneau of the truck, then came around to the cab. "I'm going with you, Lanny," she said. "Give me a hand up." For the step to the cab was high. He didn't argue. Long ago he had given up wondering about the antics or whims of the women visitors to the Lodge. But once settled in the comparative warmth of the cab and with the truck again lurching on its way, Iris felt the need to make some explanation, and his comment had given her an opening.

"I don't feel too well yet," she admitted. "Oh, not really ill, you know. But I thought I'd go down to Fredericton and wait there in the hotel for the rest of them. Do you think I'll have any trouble finding a car to take me from the village to Fredericton? If I can make it in time, I might even take the night train and go right back to Boston."

Lanny turned his face to her gravely then. No luggage, drenched clothing, a gun that would be missed. "You'd oughtn't to go this way," he reproved gently. "They'll worry about you. Think you're lost." His tone was quiet yet carried a hint of what that supposition might mean to an anxious camp. On more than one occasion he had been one of those who had hunted night and day through this elusive tracklessness in search of some one who had thought himself wise enough to leave the blazed trails.

He was a silent man ordinarily, but now he made a real effort at volubility. "Last year a couple of fellers was comin' back without any deer and pretty sore. One of 'em seen a red squirrel off the portage, shot it. And the two of 'em went in to git it. Well so help me, when they started to come out they couldn't find the portage, though they was only a little way off it. Only thing was, they still had the tree marked where the squirrel was. So one feller, he stood by the tree and the other, he just had to start from the tree and beat all around it, first in one direction, then the other, 'til he found the portage. Good thing there was two of 'em.

"The folks back there will be worried." He added pressingly, "Can't turn the truck around here, but wouldn't take me more'n twenty minutes to run back to the Lodge and tell 'em you're goin' with me."

Iris said, "Thanks, but I left a note for Dr. Harrison, saying if I weren't back by noon he could know I'd left with you." The lie sounded convincing and she went on rapidly, "I wasn't too sure I would go, you see. It would depend on how I felt. So I didn't bring any luggage, just some money. I knew I'd be down this way and could meet you if I wanted to."

Lanny was still dissatisfied, but he subsided with an inward shrug. He'd sure have some harsh things to say to his wife if she pulled any foolishness like this. He thought with vague comfort of his Dorothy, her round pale-blue eyes, her stout placidity. Now this one here had eyes like a cat's. Her wet clothes were beginning to steam in the warmth of the cab; and it almost seemed as if she was steaming too, inside, like there was something fierce and upset in her; like any moment she would snarl and the lips would curl back from her teeth.

"I caught a wolf once in a trap," he said with apparent irrelevance.

"Did you indeed," Iris replied through tight lips. Everyone had said Lanny never talked. It would be unbearable if he stepped out of character, felt the necessity of entertaining her on this interminable trip.

"We don't get wolves much any more," he went on, "but it was a hard winter and they come down from the north bold as anything."

Iris didn't answer and Lanny again fell silent. They passed the beaver dam and Lanny saw the fresh prints of a moose, the long slenderness of them pressed into the mud with the sharpness of a trowel. But he made no comment for the woman's eyes were set straight ahead. They rumbled down the hill, saw ahead of them the deceptively straight but dreaded corduroy stretch that bubbled mud from giant pores. Lanny set his gears and handled the truck as though it were a temperamental butterfly. Al-

most he thought he'd make it. Then a wheel slipped.
With a lurch and a groan the truck came to a halt, settled,
canting at a perilous angle.

Lanny sighed and said philosophically, "Now we are
here for a spell." He never wasted profanity on such
trivial and usual mishaps as this.

Iris came to then with a vengeance. "But we can't be
stuck."

"We are." They climbed from the cab and now she saw
that one great double-tired wheel had sunk to its axle in
the mud. The whole truck looked as though it might
careen on its side at any moment. "I'll go back and git
someone to help me," Lanny said placidly. "You may have
to wait a spell 'til one of the guides comes in."

Iris' face had been set, white, repelling. Now under the
pressure of this emergency she rallied, forced a glow of
animation to her face. Her eyes lifted at the corners,
smiled at him, saw him for the first time, flatteringly. "I've
heard you were the best driver in this whole section," she
said, "and I'll wager you can get out of this by yourself.
I'll help if I can, do anything you want. What would you
do," she wheedled, "if you *couldn't* find anyone else to
help?"

Lanny looked around doubtfully. "I could fasten a
chain to the wheel and fasten t'other end to that pine.
Then back the truck and pull 'er out. But it ain't so easy
to do alone."

Again Iris said, and fiercely now, "I'll help. I'm strong.
Tell me what to do." She stood facing him, challenging
him. The wind and rain beat against her face. A strand
of hair, turned brown with wetness, was plastered across

her cheek. But a vitality burned in her, an eagerness. She didn't look citified and lazy and sickly, like Mrs. Lawrence had said she was. Lanny thought of a fire that smolders under a pad of wet leaves, how it smokes at first and then darts out a thin shoot of flame. He grinned to himself. She was sure a queer one; made you think of a wolf and then of a fire. But anyways she didn't stand around whining about the wet and the cold.

She was pulling a long scarf from her pocket, was winding it around her head and neck. In that interval while she was busied, Lanny jumped back into the cab, drew out a small pint bottle. He wasn't a drinking man ordinarily, and that same bottle had reposed dustily and undisturbed in the cab for months. But now with a sort of mild surprise at himself, he took a long and comforting swig. As he climbed from the cab he saw that she was watching him. He wiped his lips and said sheepishly, "Bit by a snake. Well, let's go."

She followed him to the back of the truck, then gave a sharp little exclamation. He turned, saw her rubbing one ankle. "What's the matter?"

She looked up at him, her eyes glinting, and said, "I must have stepped on the same snake." He grinned and went obediently back to the cab. She was a one, all right. He felt suddenly sure that they'd dig the truck out. Only question was, would they get it out in time enough to suit her?

Mrs. Lawrence said worriedly, "I don't know. Her lunch has been ready a good half hour. She'll catch her death out in this rain, sick like she was last night."

"She's probably down watching Greg," Karen said. "I'll get my rain cape and go after them. Hold lunch, Mrs. Lawrence, we may not be back for a while." Tay had reached the Lodge several minutes before Karen had arrived from another direction. But he had still not removed his drenched jacket. After Mrs. Lawrence had returned to the kitchen he walked to the rack on the wall, studied it. He said slowly, "Not on the river. She's taken a gun."

He looked at Karen and she looked back at him. But all she said was, "A bad day for her first hunting try."

"Yes."

"Well," Karen said lightly, rapidly, "Greg still may have seen her, known where she was heading. Let's eliminate that first before we start off on a wild-goose chase. Nothing on the slate?"

"No."

"If she isn't with Greg, she'd be heading Beaver Dam way, then. The other sections were taken." She disappeared for a few minutes, returned with her rain cape. "All set?"

Tay still lingered irresolutely in the doorway. "The truck has gone. Left early because of the rain."

Karen's tone was still light. "Well, she didn't go with it. Her bags are still there, even her toilet things." As she preceded him down the steps she added, "Not that she needs to be burdened with powder and lipstick. Why haven't I the courage to face the world as nature made me?"

Tay's tension relaxed a little as he strode along beside her. "I don't see any powder or rouge," he teased. "The

rain has washed it off. But your lipstick certainly accentu-
ates the positive."

"Shall I go without it?"

Tay thought of a comment Iris had made. "No. I like
careless Columbines."

"Is that a compliment?"

"That's a compliment."

"Good," Karen said contentedly, "because I had no intention whatever of giving up my lipstick. I'm like that
chap in the story by—was it Leacock or Thurber or Bench-
ley? Anyway, he tossed off a glass of whisky and became
once more the perfect English gentleman! When I put on
my lipstick I can face the world."

"You face it anyway," Tay said without smiling.

They walked down the portage for a few minutes in
silence. It wasn't necessary to tell each other that in this
pouring rain they would have to seek an easier descent
than they might otherwise have done. Once they stopped
briefly in an attempt to light cigarettes, but it was futile.
The torrential downpour turned the cigarettes into sod-
den masses after the first puffs. Presently Tay said, "I hope
she's with Greg but I doubt it. Her purse is gone. And all
the money from my wallet. I think she went with the
truck."

Karen halted, walked on. But she didn't ask why Iris
should have left at all, she merely said, "Not with the
truck. Mrs. Lawrence would have known it."

"She could have picked it up along the portage. She
knew when it was coming out."

"It came out early, she'd have missed it."

"She wouldn't be staying out in this rain," he said

grimly. "She's like a cat for comfort." Not once had Iris'
actual name been spoken; it was as though they were con-
tent to use merely the anonymous pronoun.

"Then so are we." Karen tried to laugh. "We both
came back."

"Did you come back because of the rain?"

Karen gave up all pretense then. "No, because I was
uneasy after last night. But the rain was a good excuse to
give Mrs. Lawrence, particularly since she'd gone to the
bother of putting up a lunch for me. Now the poor soul
is getting another meal, a hot one."

They left the portage, struck through the soaking underbrush to the edge of the bluff and scrambled down it.
There were fewer rocks here and the slope was comparatively gentle, but the rain had turned the earth to a slipping quagmire of mud and pine needle. By the shore the
tall grasses stood swordlike and desolate to the rain, only
their tips bending. The river boiled and tore down its
course, submerging most of its boulders, showing white
teeth against those that still projected. On the opposite
shore the colors of the woods had vanished; the gray veil
of the rain enveloped them in an opaque haze.

"Shall we divide forces? You go one way and I the
other?"

"No," Tay said, "not yet at least. Greg would be working back toward the Lodge. He couldn't hold his footing
in this current now, and he's alone unless she joined him."

"He might still be in the dugout."

"Not in this rain," he objected again. "The current is
too strong for a pole. He'd be carried down to the Mirimichi and he'd know that." They turned and started along

the shore toward the Lodge again. They were wearing, wood boots, unprotected against the water; and again and again they sank to their knees in the small new inlets created by the rain and river. But soon they had turned the bend, could see the boathouse. The stern of the dug-out rocked wildly in the stream, but its bow was still uncertainly caught between two rocks on the bank.

As they drew nearer they could see Gregory too.

"The idiot!" Karen exclaimed. "How can he sleep in all this rain!" Her voice sharpened. "Or do you suppose he's hurt his bad leg somehow?" But Tay was running now, running with giant strides that carried him over boulder and inlet, with flailing arms that struck aside the overhanging bushes. Karen's slower course demanded most of her attention. Even so she was aware when she could glance up occasionally, that Tay had reached Gregory, that he was kneeling beside him.

He knelt so long. Too long. Her breath caught in her throat.

Now Tay was rising, coming toward her. Her heart was a pounding drum in her breast as he reached her, gripped her shoulders, put his arms about her in a sudden passion of tenderness. It was the tenderness that was frightening, that told her; not his words. For at first he only said, "Karen. Oh, Karen."

And then somehow, a little later, she was huddled down beside Gregory too, her hand resting on Gregory's hand, her spent, anguished eyes looking across him to where Tay crouched. And the rain poured and poured and was a dreadful sheet of coldness over them and over Gregory. "What happened?" she asked finally, drearily.

"Are you all right now?"

"I'm all right."

"Then look the other way a few minutes, darling. Look at the river and don't think about anything."

And Karen looked at the river and didn't think about anything. It was easy, he needn't have told her. She looked too at the old gramophone, with the water splattering high from the record that lay there. She moved a little without rising, reached out and lifted the record so that she could see it. *From the Land of the Sky-Blue Water.* But that was silly. The water wasn't blue, nor the sky either. Alma Gluck. And it was strange that a voice could go on and on long after its singer was gone. Stranger still that an ancient, cracked record should preserve the semblance of its identity through two generations that had disappeared: her mother and her brother. "And I came to her Lodge at dawning." She remembered the words. "I wooed her with my flute. She is sick for the Sky-Blue Water, the captive maid is mute."

Greg and his mother had been alike, loving the simple melodies with their simple, sentimental words; had been alike too in their physical resemblance, their blondness, their sturdy bodies. But her mother's sturdiness had not been proof against an automobile accident. And now, Greg.

"Karen." She turned. "Greg must have fallen down the bluff. His spine was badly injured."

"Broken?" Her voice was harsh, wanting him to use the harsh word, let it fall as a final period.

"Yes. But it was his temple landing against this stone

that—did it." Tay added quickly, "He couldn't have been conscious, only during his fall, perhaps."

Karen struggled to her feet now and Tay rose also. "Why would he ever try to climb the bluff *here?* He couldn't possibly make the last few feet and he'd have known it!" Her tone rose. "He wouldn't have tried to climb with rubber boots on, anyway. And even one of those is off. It doesn't make sense!"

"It doesn't make sense but it must have happened. He couldn't have been injured this badly, here on the shore." Tay's eyes sought the bluff, ranged up and down it. But if originally there had been any marks of that fall, rain and wind had washed them out, at least temporarily. Later perhaps, they would find a broken bush, a gully dug by a trailing foot, not rain. But at the moment nothing was to be seen from this distance. He looked at her searchingly.

"Can you think of any reason at all why Greg would have tried to make the bluff here?"

"Yes." She was blunt. "If he were needed badly. Suddenly. But even then," Karen repeated, "he'd have known he couldn't climb those last yards."

"Unless someone helped him. Or tried to, and failed."

They stared at each other. Then Tay opened his palm, held it out to her, shielding it from the direct downpour with his other hand. A few strands of wool lay there, strands every color of the rainbow. "They were between the fingers of one hand," he said quietly.

"Her scarf!"

Karen's lips trembled for the first time in long moments. "She was with him and let this happen?" she asked pitifully. "Why should she try to help him and then let him go? Not even tell Mrs. Lawrence! Tay, she must be ill somewhere." She swallowed, her voice steadied. "Maybe she was lots more ill than you thought last night and is wandering around delirious. What happened?" she cried again, wildly.

For a time Tay was silent. Then he said slowly, "Perhaps she *was* ill, called to him. Perhaps she tried to help him up the last stretch with the scarf. And couldn't hold on. As you say, she may be wandering around now, afraid to come back to the Lodge and tell us."

Karen made a valiant effort. "Go and find her, Tay. Now. I'll go back to the Lodge and give the gun signal for the others. But oh, God, the truck is gone!" Her hands still held the record clutched to her chest. Her fingertips drummed nervously on it, soundless under the even louder beating of the rain. Tay's eyes fastened on her hands, on the disk she held.

"Karen," he said suddenly, "did Iris ever sing for Greg? I mean, especially? When I wasn't there?" His face darkened. "Or for *you?*"

Even under her confusion and despair the utter irrelevance of his question struck her dumb for a moment. But her chaotic mind refused to speculate and she answered obediently, "She sang for Greg once. I missed it, came in just too late."

"When?"

"That afternoon you decided to come to the Lodge. Two days before we left."

"What did she sing?"

"Oh, God, Tay, I don't remember." Her eyes pleaded with him to release her from this senseless examination, pleaded with him to see again Gregory's body between them. But his voice probed on.

"You don't remember. Then you knew once, Greg told you. Try to remember, Karen, it's important."

She struggled from her stupor at the urgency of his voice. "*Herodiade.* '*Il est doux, il est bon.*' I remember that."

"Nothing else? Greg liked the old-timers, college songs."

She shook her head. "I don't remember."

"*The Star-Spangled Banner? Home, Sweet Home?*"

She lifted her chin then. "Yes, she sang that. *Home, Sweet Home.* I remember because Greg said she sang it without the piano. Beautifully. Tay, can't we go back now? I can't bear to leave Greg lying here in this rain any longer. And I *have* to see Dad!" And now she broke and her weeping was as wild and desolate as the rain about them.

Tay took the record from her, laid it on the bench. He took her in his arms again for a brief moment, with a gentleness, an impersonality that might have been Greg's. But as he held her, his eyes did not look down. They rested unseeingly on the swirling current of the river.

Karen could not know why he had returned so early, so unexpectedly from what should have been a day's hunting, rain or no rain. He had returned because of a Sunday Supplement which he had seen before he left the Lodge; which he had seen and left purposely behind him, sure that in the boredom of a day alone at the Lodge Iris would eventually find and read it. The afternoon would have been theirs for a full and final reckoning. Alone.

For Iris had been right: Tay had given up hope that his own elaborate and melodramatic trap would ever function. And he had come to pin his last hope on Ester, Ester who represented the tortoiselike progress of the mysterious machine behind her. The hare and the tortoise, he had thought, and had not felt mirthful. The Washington tortoise, at least, must have felt fairly sure of its eventual success. For when he had talked with Ester from Fredericton she had agreed without demur to the Sunday Supplement article. Someone would write it, she promised, and a few prints would be struck off with the collaboration of the newspaper. At least two copies of that very exclusive issue should reach the Lodge eventually; if not this Sunday, then next. Ester's voice had been quiet, a little pitying. They didn't need him then, they had never needed him.

He looked down at Gregory's body in the humility of despair. "Venom spreads inward too much." But it had spread outward too; it had spread and lapped around Gregory. And when Karen knew, would it spread about her too? Not striking her physically—that could never happen now—but poisoning the brightness and candor of her, the charity and belief and eagerness? Some arrogance in Tay whimpered and expired, finally. He listened, as though with its death he must physically hear the thundering shatter of his whole ego.

As though she had read his thoughts, Karen stirred in his arms, turned, looked up at him. "Tay," she whispered, "don't feel too badly, even if Iris couldn't help Gregory." She stared at him with her eyes wide. "She must be ill. Go and find her." She broke away from him with a last look at her brother, and started along the shore. As he caught up with her she went on, hurriedly, mumblingly, "You'll have to catch the truck anyway. Or go after it. Can you use Ben's bicycle part of the way? We'll have to have the truck."

Back on the portage Tay said, "I may not come back at all, Karen. I may have to follow Iris clear to Boston, because I'm sure she's heading that way. Don't say anything to Mrs. Lawrence until I'm out of the Lodge. I won't be seven minutes and I don't want to be held up with long explanations."

"You'll need money if she took yours."

"Just give me a little cash. They'll trust me with a car in the village and they'll take a check in Fredericton if I have to follow her that far. Tell Ben I may have to ditch his bicycle along the portage but I'll fix it up with him later. I'll have them send up two trucks and men from the village. You and your father can carry on from there all right, even if I don't have time to make any other arrangements for you?"

"Yes."

Tay wasn't seven minutes at the Lodge, he was less than five. She followed him back to the porch and he looked down, saw the grief, the question in her eyes; saw the confidence too, that trusted in him; that was too proud to voice that question. He caught at her hands hurriedly.

"Karen," he said, "in my big suitcase there's a copy of the Sunday paper. Look at the extra supplement. It's just one feature article. Then you'll know—nearly everything." His arms held her briefly, despairingly. "And try not to hate me. I love you so much."

"I couldn't hate you."

"No matter what?"

"No matter what," she repeated on a final, unshakable inflection. Then he was gone.

Karen brought the gun from the living room, and kneeling on the porch, she steadied the weapon on the railing, pointing it at a high, skyward angle. And in another moment the ominous thunder of it rolled up and down the river, reechoed from the farther shore.

13

Iris sat back in the train. She had made it with a little time to spare, even though the Fredericton stores had been closed and she had been unable to buy a change of clothing. That didn't matter. Even her heated cheeks and the clammy coldness of her feet and hands didn't matter. She had made the train. Lanny had found a car and a driver for her in the village and they had done the sixty miles to Fredericton in an hour and eleven minutes, against the driving rain. For a part of the way it had seemed that the Mirimichi was racing with them, hurtling between its banks with a secret message from the tributary river that flanked the Lodge . . . Once she had looked back, seized with the fantastic idea that Gregory's dugout might come bobbing by at any moment, might outpace her to the train, blazing in some mystic way the banner of his death. She had felt an unreasonable and sagging relief when the road turned, took them from sight of the Mirimichi.

So she had made the train, unhalted and unquestioned, and the train had been a friend as long as it was moving through the night; but now it had stopped and the minutes were crawling. At last she rose, her impatience burning in her and went out to the platform. There was fog here as well as murk, but she could distinguish a brakeman's lantern and she called to him.

"Where are we and how long are we here?"

"Fredericton Junction, lady. We don't leave 'til nine forty-five."

"Nearly two hours?" She almost screamed at him but his voice came back with cheery nonchalance.

"That's right. Customs inspector will be along any minute. Better not get out 'til he's seen you." The lantern went on, was swallowed up in the night and the rain-gloom of the station.

Almost two hours.

What if the storm had driven Tay back to the Lodge early? A bicycle, a pedestrian even, could make almost as good time as the truck on that boggy portage. But she had been secure in the knowledge that he still would not have)een able to catch the night train, under any circumstances. Now of course that possibility loomed, if he could reach the Junction by car; if he knew of this prolonged wait.

She returned to her compartment and presently the inspector appeared. His surprise and doubt at her lack of luggage didn't daunt her; and even though she was not forced to make any explanations she chose to. Sudden illness may not be convincing but it is unarguable. And she found as she had guessed, that the Littlefield name was a potent one. Almost she had used it when she had begged for a compartment, but it hadn't proved necessary. The train was not crowded as it would be a few days from now when the fishing season ended.

"Yessir," the inspector said finally, rising with an obvious reluctance, "that family has been back and forth for years, way before my time." But his eyes were still curious, still wondered at her disheveled, unescorted state. She looked up at him prettily, challenging his wonder.

"Oh, they'll never forgive me," she said lightly, "but I'd never forgive myself if they missed getting deer. And I'm much better off at home than being an invalid underfoot in the woods. By the way, does the train always stop here this long, or is there some trouble tonight?"

"It's a regular stop."

Then Tay might know, might remember, might be driving on wildly toward her through the night. Nonsense, that was ridiculous. It would demand too many sets of circumstances dovetailing together too neatly. "There's a store across the way," the inspector said as he moved toward the door. "All kinds of things from stoves to stockings. Well, maybe not stoves. But it keeps open for this train if you want anything." His look comprehended the one handbag she carried.

Iris didn't want to leave the security of her compartment. She had the feeling that within it she was somehow safe. But common sense told her that she should seize the opportunity of acquiring a toothbrush, handkerchiefs, perhaps dry stockings. She looked at her boots ruefully. They were well oiled, but when she had been forced to step into the river grasses, the water had overflowed their tops, soaking the inside linings. Fortunate indeed that they had been too large unless worn with extra socks. With one pair of dry stockings, it should still be possible to get into them in the morning, however boardlike they dried, however much they had shrunk.

She stepped to the station platform and looked cautiously up and down its misty length. Only two passengers had cared to leave the warmth of the train for the dubious pleasure of strolling the rain-swept platform; and neither resembled Tay. Across the tracks at a little distance she saw the blue and eerie glow of dim neon lights that marked the store. At its door she paused, glanced in against the soot that crusted the glass. The proprietor leaned over a counter, chatting with a lone customer whose features were clear and unfamiliar. Iris stepped in.

A half hour later, her compartment door bolted, she was examining her purchases. The berth had been made up in her absence and she spread the different articles on it: a cheap and garish raincoat, a bright blue scarf, toothbrush, handkerchief, cotton stockings, a box of crackers, candy. She had deliberately left her long cashmere scarf in the store, dropping it behind a counter when the proprietor's back was turned. She never wanted to see it again, even though she might miss tomorrow the soft spongy warmth of it; for the raincoat was thin and her tweed jacket might not dry thoroughly overnight. As she forced herself to eat some of the food, she nodded with the first satisfaction she had felt since the train had halted. The clothing ensemble was hardly one that Tay would be looking for, if by some wild chance he still made the train.

He had not made it so far, she was sure of that. But there were still four minutes left to go. She switched off the lights, thrust the shade higher up the window. Her face pressed to the glass, her eyes roamed up and down the foggy platform, keeping a particular watch on the parking space beyond the tracks. That space was invisible in detail, but headlights would stab even through the fog. She glanced at her watch, listened. Presently the train rumbled, shook; the locomotive coughed warningly. With a drag and a reluctant jerk the wheels moved; seemed to slip back; halted again and gripped the rails. The carriage lurched forward.

Iris pulled down the shade and turned on the lights. In the small mirror by the window she caught a glance of her reflection, was about to look away with her usual indifference. Then she paused, startled; leaned forward.

The lips were not coral now. They were gray-white, drawn back high and square over her gums. From nose to mouth, two unfamiliar and hateful lines printed a parenthesis. Only the eyes were darker than usual, their pupils still distended from peering against the night gloom. In that pallid face they stood out, harsh and menacing, like black slits in a white mask. The face looked old, old, old.

Iris' hands shook. She reached out, and for the first time opened the compact that had been an unused accessory of the handbag. She must put some make-up on, now. Even though it would immediately be removed. She wouldn't dare close her eyes against the darkness, leaving them with that last image of a tarnished and aging face, the face of a stranger . . . There was a squeal of car brakes outside in the night. Confused shouts followed, shouts that were muffled in the rain and wind and the turning of the wheels as the train pulled slowly from the station.

Iris did not hear them. The compartment was warm and bright, a small island of security above the first comfortable grinding of the wheels. Her face close to the tiny mirror of the compact, she was drawing a mouth, a woman's red and tender and human mouth . . .

The morning was still furious with rain; and even though her head felt heavy and her feet were leaden, Iris surveyed both the storm and her reflection with satisfac-

tion. The raincoat enveloped her and the blue cotton
scarf, wound peasant fashion about her face, almost ob-
scured her features. Reasonable enough against the nor'-
easter that was afflicting Boston. She looked, she thought,
dowdy, insignificant and practical. Long before the train
was due in the station, long before the porter would think
to rouse her, she left the compartment and started edging
her way toward the forward carriage. Twice she dodged
the conductor by stepping into ladies' rooms that were just
beginning to fill with sleepy, irritable women, listlessly
intent on making a sketchy morning toilette.

Unencumbered with luggage, she was the first passenger to leave the train. And she moved quickly, holding
her steps to a brisk, reasonable walk that still covered
ground. Two porters glanced after her sharply; so did the
conductor from his harassed stand by a certain carriage
down the line. All three looked away. She couldn't be
the one.

Once in the North Station, Iris abandoned all caution
and ran toward the taxi rank. She jumped into a cab and
threw a bill to the driver. It fluttered down to the seat
beside him and he glanced back at her with dawning surprise, from the impressive bill to the very unimpressive
raincoat and scarf. Still, you never could tell these days.
"Get going," she said, and though her voice was low it
was peremptory, cold. "It's all yours if you get me there as
fast as possible." And she gave the address.

The four men were still arguing by the train. "Listen,
mister," one of the porters was saying soothingly, "I'm telling you the lady in my car didn't have any luggage, not a
snitch. Not even a paper bag, only her purse. So how

could she be wearing something different than what she had on last night? She just ain't come out, that's all."

The tall man with the tense face was still dissatisfied; but he gave each of the porters a bill. "Keep on the lookout a while longer," he ordered and they nodded, moving away. Then he turned to the conductor. "Let's go," he said harshly. "The train's in and it's past schedule time. You have a right to open any compartment now whether the occupant answers or not. My wife is ill, perhaps delirious. I must be sure she's actually left the train, that she hasn't wandered into some empty compartment and bolted the door."

"Well, all right." But the conductor was still dubious. "One of the parties had a big night," he warned. "Don't be surprised if you hear language." He added apologetically as they started through a carriage, "Sorry I couldn't oblige last night. But if we was to wake up every lady that a gentleman took a notion to talk to, well, we would be getting into trouble."

The tall man didn't answer and under the pressure of that unsmiling tension, the conductor found his own steps hurrying. But he was experienced enough, and now as he paused by a compartment his tone took on a new authority. "You'll stand back out of sight, please," he ordered curtly. He had eyed this passenger closely, particularly the roomy pockets of that hunting jacket. Maybe the man was looking for a sick wife and maybe he was looking for a two-timing girl friend. You never could tell, even with a real gentleman. And he didn't want a shooting fracas on his hands. "Out of sight, please," he repeated.

Iris opened the front door, closed it behind her. For a long moment she stood in the big hall, listening to the silence of the house, feeling it well up around her in a convincing emptiness. Even more convincing was the snow of circulars that lay on the floor, pushed through from the letter-slot. She knelt, saw that among them was mail for Hulda and Dana, none for Ester. It was unlikely that Ester was back though. She would never have left this untidy accumulation lying here. But it was just as well to be certain.

She glanced through the downstairs first, every room; called loudly down the cellar stairs. There was no answer. Rapidly as she moved, she became conscious of the cold of the house; and looking at the thermostat in the hall she saw that it was still set at a low point. Ester wouldn't be here then, Ester who loved her "warm radiators and her comforts." But Iris didn't halt until she had made a complete though flying tour of the whole house.

It was hers, she was alone in it.

She paused only long enough to kick off the stiff boots that had begun to blister her heels; then in stockinged feet she hurried down to the music room and stared around. The window drapes were closely drawn and the rain-swept morning had made no headway against this gloom. One of the small wall sconces would give just enough light to see by, without advertising its presence in a house apparently empty. She switched it on and the room looked sedately if dimly back at her, the piano linen-shrouded; the panels secret in their brocade.

Common sense told her that she probably had hours in which to make a leisurely search for that hidden space; but

common sense had been faltering ever since the train had
paused at the Junction and she had accepted the possibility
of immediate pursuit. So now her eyes fixed one wall as
though her very gaze would force it to open to her. If
there were a door, it must be down here, near the terrace,
for on the other side of the partition the coat closet
reached to about this spot. She ran out to the corridor and
confirmed that guess. Then she returned. Yes. One of
these four panels must be the door. But which?

Memory berated her. Of course. The hall mirror
would tell the story. She went up the stairs, paused on the
landing and looked down. The mirrored reflection was
even; there was no illusion of a caving wall. She was puzzled but not disturbed. The last time she had seen this
reflection the wall had still been out of line. But Tay had
been with her from that moment on, so he could have had
no hand in the matter. The door had shut of itself perhaps; or more likely, Dana in her clumsy sweeping had
backed against it. But she would take notice of nothing,
that one, let alone a door that was not actually open,
merely unlatched. Iris' puzzlement was swept away by
almost immediate triumph. It didn't matter anyway. *The
mirror reflected only one edge of only one panel.* That
edge, then, must be the part of the door that opened. It
remained only to take a landmark, as it were, by which to
identify the panel that was reflected.

By leaning far over the rail, a further portion of the
room came into her view and she could see the needlepoint hassock . . .

She had kicked the hassock aside and now her fingers
were roaming the panel's edge, hopefully at first, then

feverishly. She paused, took a long breath, fought panic down. The house was warm enough now, in all conscience; her forehead was burning. The catch or spring that opened the door was here, must be here. And suddenly her palm, not her fingers, found it; her palm resting with tired pressure against the brocade, feeling a projecting something that had been concealed under the rounded padding of the brocade.

As she cautiously lifted her hand there was a little click and the panel opened, much as a compact or a cigarette case opens under just such a similar, casual pressure. The door swung inward, and before she released her shoulder from it she waited to see if it were hung on any self-closing device. But it remained half open.

She stepped forward into the room.

It was so then. It had really happened. The trap was here, the cruelty that had set a snare.

She had felt a dim half-regret the night before; had, for a few minutes, turned and beaten her fists on the pillow, trying to shut out the sight of a bluff and a river. Now, staring with glazed eyes at a machine and a cabinet, her right palm tingled, feeling again the coldness of a jagged stone. If she had had a sure knowledge of this room, she thought with an even colder, deadlier malice, that palm would have lifted, not once; but again and again and again. No, she didn't regret the stone. There was only bitterness and rage for the one thing left undone: that she had carried the gun to no purpose; that Tay had walked unscathed "west from Springy Landing"; that he had no doubt returned unscathed.

Returned? Common sense was again swamped as she

glanced at her watch, saw that she had been in the house a good eight minutes; and one of those precious minutes had already been wasted here.

Resolutely she stepped toward the machine; only one step, for the room was very narrow. Cabinet, machine and two chairs crowded it. Even the metal wastebasket seemed out-size. A record lay on the turntable and to one side was a blank memo pad. Looking down at the record she thought that the wax surface was scored. But the glow from the music room was dim. She glanced up, turned on the unshaded bulb that hung above her head. Yes, the record *was* scored; it had been used. There was a good chance then that it was the latest disk, the one that had recorded the songs which she had sung for Gregory . . .

The playback device looked ordinary enough, and if it worked she would listen to this record. But it didn't really matter anyway, for she intended to destroy all the disks; this one, and those others in the cabinet that she wouldn't have time to listen to. But now as she leaned forward to adjust the needle-arm, the light struck across the memo pad that she had pushed to one side. It wasn't blank after all, it seemed, for in this brighter glare of the overhead bulb, she could see the faint close lines scribbled in a hard lead that had dented the paper but scarcely darkened it.

Dear Tay,

If your latest idea works out, the article I mean, you'll probably be leaving camp before you originally expected. And I may not be here though I hope to be back the 16th if a certain ship docks on schedule. I'll be bringing someone you never heard of, but you'll be interested. Anyway, the record on the table is my apology. I think I understand a little better now how you feel. I'll have to apologize to Toni too. He'll rave when he finds I pulled this on him when he wasn't looking. Hoist by his own petard, so to speak!

And Tay, don't be too discouraged. You sounded so over the phone. Remember that things do work out but not always in the way we plan. Sometimes we're better off in the long run.

E.

E. E meant nothing to Iris. Neither did Toni nor a petard nor the arrival of a certain ship. She touched the lever on the machine and glanced again at her watch. She had been in the house thirteen minutes now. The needle moved, gathered momentum. A man's voice said:

"Like I told you, there was a two-day march back to the Nip camp and the Hiros thought they might as well make good use of the time. They knew that somewhere along the way there was a missionary family holed up with a batch of Moros . . ."

As the voice went on, Iris stepped back, braced her stockinged feet in the thick carpet. ". . . Poor kid, even at five, even born in the jungle, she knew her American songs, just like a parrot would."

"Oh, my God," a woman's voice commented, a strangely familiar voice. Iris leaned forward.

"Yeah, only He wasn't looking just at that moment. When Tay saw her, the kid's head was in one ditch and the rest of her in another."

"Her hair was in pigtails, yellow pigtails. And they weren't mussed . . ."

Ester. It really was Ester. But Iris did not move. She stood frozen as the record went on like the whine of an interminable nightmare. Her ears heard and recorded with an inexorable fidelity as had the needle; but her mind was closed to everything but the crash and thunder within it. The seaweed no longer drifted and anchored according to its whim. It was lashed by the storm, smitten by the waves, ripped tentacle from delicate tentacle. The fragments of it submerged, clung to the shore, were dragged outward again by the remorseless inhalation of the breakers.

"And being a doctor, maybe he was so jittery it didn't strike him that for severed arteries a tourniquet might be more useful than a bandage."

The needle spun to the edge of the platter and the record fell silent. Iris reached out mechanically and stilled the table. Against the silence and the stillness she spoke loudly, absurdly. "I must think," she said, "I must think."

She picked up her purse, groped inside it, found a cigarette. She scratched a match, lit the cigarette; flipped the still-lighted match into the metal wastebasket. There was a crackle, a roar; and a sheet of flame shot up from the container. Iris leaped back. Her shoulder struck the door, lunged against it. It closed with a sharp click. An acrid billow of smoke filled the room, dimming on an instant the light of the one bulb. The handbag dropped to the floor, its contents spilling.

She whirled, caught at the door handle, wrenched at it frantically. The door didn't move. She twisted the handle back and forth, pulled with all her strength. The panel did not even tremble. The lunge of her weight would be worse than useless for the door opened inward, yet in her panic she lunged desperately. Finally she slid to the floor, whimpering.

But the crackle and the flame had died. The basket had contained the brief blaze, it had not spread to the room. She was hardly conscious of the fact, for she still coughed with the stench of the smoke and her eyes felt red and blinded. She sat up weakly, leaning against the door, and tried to peer through the haze. What was it she had planned to do? She had planned to think. How could one think in this terror, this suffocation? She pressed her palms against her streaming eyes.

There were no windows, but there must be concealed ventilation somewhere. Tay wouldn't have built a room without it. Yet though the smoke had eddied upwards a little, it still hung menacing, bolsterlike, almost without motion in the currentless air of the room. Perhaps the ventilator had been shuttered from the outside when the house was closed? No, no, she mustn't even admit that possibility, it was ridiculous. Yet it could be so. Too many things could be so.

She coughed again, half strangling. Her lungs labored.

Could there be any worse death than slow suffocation? A sword, a stone, even starvation were sheer mercy in comparison. Not that she would suffocate, of course. Tay was following her, would be here any moment. She tried to see her watch but her eyes were useless. The minutes that had spun by so fast were crawling now, moving on snail-like feet. What if Tay *weren't* following her? What if he had accepted Mrs. Lawrence's report at its face value, was preparing to return in his own leisurely time and fashion, contemptuously sure that she would be waiting here; or contemptuously indifferent if she had vanished for good? Her mind was heavy, dazed, unable to cope with a possibility that would once have loomed as unexpected good luck, but which now shook her with physical terror. Tay *must* come back, must come soon. She would face any death, but not like this, not like a rat in a trap . . .

Or Ester. Ester had been an enemy while Iris had listened to that strange record. Now Ester was a friend. And Ester was perhaps coming back the sixteenth. Was that today or tomorrow? When she had read the note, Iris had been blandly sure that it was tomorrow, for she remembered now that she had had no fear of encountering Ester; only fear of Tay. But her eyes were so poor without glasses and the penciling had been so light. Perhaps Ester had written a fifteen, not a sixteen. And today was the fifteenth, wasn't it? Or was it?

Iris coughed again and her mouth sagged.

No, it wasn't the fifteenth; she might as well admit it. For she had read the paper yesterday and for the first time in two weeks had glanced at a date. Sunday, the thirteenth. Today was only the fourteenth. She couldn't count on Ester, only on Tay. And he wasn't coming either. If he had by any chance taken that same train, he would have been here long before this . . . A sharp swordlike pain stabbed her side and suddenly it was sheer agony to draw a breath. This was it, then. Suffocation. Queer too, because a moment or two before, she had imagined that the room was growing lighter, that the smoke was thinning.

Her tweed suit was still dank and clammy and the room was icy cold, but Iris struggled out of her jacket, sprawled to the floor again. Her body was burning. She husbanded her breath, breathing lightly and shallowly from the top of her lungs, trying to avoid the dark pool of agony that followed each full inhalation. Her mind clouded. She was climbing a twisting way on Montmartre, she was climbing a jungle path, she was climbing a bluff. They were so steep but it was only a matter of power; in this case, power over herself. She willed her feet to keep moving and they did. But up and down, up and down in one spot, not advancing. Leaving her to the mercy of the thing that was crawling behind her, so slowly yet so inexorably . . .

Tay came into the hall and closed the door behind him with no attempt at furtiveness. Its sound was, rather, a loud challenge throughout the house. Without pausing, he started down the corridor that led to the music room, saw without surprise that a dim glow came from the doorway. The library telephone rang. He hesitated; then ignoring it, he stepped forward over the threshold. The music room was empty, but the needlepoint hassock had been moved from its usual place and a pair of gloves were sprawled on its flowered surface.

The telephone rang more and more insistently.

He was tempted not to answer it, but it might be Karen. On that mere possibility he turned and his steps quickened as he crossed the corridor and picked up the receiver of the telephone.

"That you, Tay?" It was Ester's voice.

"Yes."

"How have things gone?"

"Badly. You couldn't have called at a worse moment. She ran away from camp and I followed her to the house. She's here but I haven't seen her yet. I just this second got in. Please don't keep me. I'm sure she's in the little room."

"Wait! I *must* keep you."

"No. I tell you she's in the record room with the door shut."

"Then let her stay there. Tay, don't go near her until I get there. It's important. Urgently important."

"Greg is dead—and I wouldn't be surprised if she had a hand in it," he said bluntly. "I'm not waiting for anyone or anything."

There was a little pause, then Ester's voice said quietly, "I'm terribly sorry about that, for all of you. But it doesn't change things. You will not go near her until I get to the house. That is an order. I mean—consider it as an order from the department I represent." She listened for a long minute to the first flow of profanity she had ever heard Tay indulge in; if half his predictions came true, the department would wither away adverbially at the roots and the country would lie in adjectival ruins. Suddenly he paused, not from lack of breath but because memory had flung at him, like a dash of cold water, that moment of abject humility that he had felt when he stood beside Greg's body.

Ester seized that opportunity. "Fine," she said calmly, "you sound okay. We'll be there in twenty minutes at the outside." And she hung up.

Tay sat back in his chair and filled his pipe from the desk humidor. He puffed stormily, but with the third puff he removed the pipe, stared at it critically. Something was wrong with the tobacco, or else someone in the neighborhood was burning not only leaves but some acrid-smelling rubbish as well. That must be it, for he remembered now that he had unconsciously noted that odor as, and even before, he had entered the house. He sat back and finished the pipe, his eyes never passing beyond the range of the one door to the music room.

Presently the soft hall chimes began to sound. It was only then that he left his post, flung the front door open and stepped back to allow Ester and her companion to enter. The three of them went to the library and the spate of words mounted for ten minutes; was only checked when Tay lifted his head with a sudden frown and stood up. "Whatever is burning is inside the house!" The telephone rang as he spoke and he thrust the receiver at Ester. "Take it. If it's Miss Littlefield, ask her to please call later." And he strode toward the music room.

Iris awoke, stared around her uncomprehendingly, then with a dull memory whose outlines eluded her. Escape. It was too slow, this escape, and while she waited she had to breathe, she thought complainingly. She *must* breathe. Already she had forgotten the futility of her earlier struggle and now she staggered somehow to her feet, and with weak fingers lifted the door handle. The door swung open, mildly, casually; and Iris stumbled into the music room. Almost immediately she slumped to the floor again, one arm flung over the needlepoint hassock. Somewhere in the muffled distance a telephone rang sharply; it was halted suddenly in the midst of its insistence. Like her breath, she thought disinterestedly. It was too much bother to move her head so her half-open stare remained on the outflung arm and hand. It was so grimy, so soiled, that hand. But it must be hers because the diamond clung to it.

There was a step in the doorway and Tay stood there. He didn't come forward. He just stood, unmoving.

Finally he said, "Smashed all the records, did you?"

"Every one." And she had meant to smash them, so it must be so. She always did what she meant to do. "The fire is out," she offered vaguely, "all out. Such a big fire for such a little basket."

He ignored that. "You didn't need to smash them," he said clearly. "The songs you sang to Greg aren't there."

Her look was stupid on his but she was trying to understand; not caring very much. He moved then, not toward her but toward the paneled door. He glanced in, confirming her comment about the fire, then stepped back again. And he rested his hand on one of the brocade panels. "You didn't smash them, Iris," he said, "but it wouldn't have mattered anyway. You flattered us. The machine is not quite that automatic. Did you think it functioned day and night whether anyone worked it or not? Well, it doesn't. Someone has to press this button to start it recording. And I don't suppose either you or Greg did that."

She didn't understand, except that something she had done had not been necessary.

"You had to kill Greg though, of course. I can see that." He waited.

"Yes," she smiled, "naturellement." And coughed.

Tay stared at her. "I suppose this phony act means you're going to plead insanity. It won't work, Iris. You may as well get up. I have no intention of falling for any part of it. *We* have no intention," he added with an impersonality that held no triumph, only a curt distaste.

She coughed again, a hard dry cough that distorted her face. "Peste!" she whispered wonderingly, "I can breathe no better in here either."

Tay threw another light switch, looked at her searchingly in the soft brilliance that now flooded the room.
Then he moved quickly to her side, knelt. "Ester!" he called.
Iris eyes were open but they stared beyond him. They
were heavy on Ester as the woman came through the doorway, but the eyes did not blink or wonder.

Ester's eyes didn't blink or wonder either. She said
composedly, "The old dodge?"

"No, we'll have to get her upstairs at once. She has
pneumonia."

Down the hall near the stairs, the slim woman in black
sat underneath the heavy mirror. Her feet were primly
planted in front of her and her hands clutched a shabby
purse without moving. Only her eyes shuttled back and
forth, taking in the heavy color of the great Chinese rug,
avidly glimpsing a corner of the living room toward which
a delicate iron balustrade descended. With the curtains
drawn like this and with the rain outside, the house was
like a great cavern under the sea, she thought nervously.
And she stifled a little cry when a strange shape suddenly
appeared around the bend of a corridor and started toward
her. But it wasn't a sea monster. It was only Dr. Harrison
carrying a woman who lay limply against him.

The woman's arm, bare to the elbow in its light blouse,
thrust out beyond his shoulder; described a stiff arc as it
passed close to the women in black. The fingers were
soiled, but above their sootiness the huge diamond ring
glittered immaculately. Now Dr. Harrison had turned,
and his wife's face was brought into view. Her eyes were
open and they stared straight into the eyes of the woman
in black. Fixed.

"Eh bien, Marie," Iris whispered, "comment ça va? Et Fritz, dites-moi—" The voice died away, the eyes marched on, still open as the man mounted the stairs.

The nostrils of the woman in black quivered, dilated, but she did not speak and her feet remained motionless. Only her head bent in an imperceptible nod as Ester paused and looked at her with lifted eyebrows. Ester didn't speak either. She went on swiftly, passing on the broad stairway the man and his burden. The eyes of the watcher in the hall raised to see those last two vanish in the obscurity of the upstairs gloom.

The man's face had been almost as dreadful as that of 'Ris, for his granite features had held no expression. None at all. Not anger nor pity nor hate. Nothing. They had passed beyond her sight now and she was glad. They were strangers, both of them, she thought firmly. She would do her duty, make her declaration and go, secure in the peace that could never be shattered again. But her lip trembled. It was a beautiful ring; it would have meant many charities, many masses . . .

She throttled the thought, uncertain of its worthiness; and her hand slipped into her purse, closed around the beads that lay there. The hall was quiet again. The eyes of the woman in black were quiet now too, downcast. Only her lips moved soundlessly.

Ester picked up the receiver of the telephone and glanced at the library clock. It wasn't really too late in the evening; it just seemed late, perhaps because Toni was yawning so loudly on the leather couch, or because the whole house was so dim and subdued, or because occasionally she could see one of the nurses whisk through the hall on night-soft steps.

"Hello," she said. And after a moment, "I'm sorry to put you off again, Miss Littlefield, but Mrs. Harrison is very ill. It's pneumonia . . . Yes, very. Dr. Harrison is upstairs now with Dr. Kennard and Dr. Beauchamp, and I wouldn't want to disturb him . . . At the Junction? Yes. I'll surely tell him. You'll be here in the morning." She replaced the receiver. "She's a saint if she's really sorry," she commented dryly to Toni.

It was pleasant here under the canopy of the trees. It was secluded, safe. As the woods darkened she breathed more and more easily. When that one thin ray of sunlight vanished it would be night; and she had always been able to sleep at night, as Marie had once pointed out. Tonight wouldn't be any different, would it? She suppressed a little stir of uneasiness. She felt more comfortable every moment and it would be stupid to mumble a confession and regret it later; equally stupid to weaken oneself by questioning, even inwardly, the whole structure of a life. Besides, there were those lines she had always remembered from her English textbook, lines about a man who had been killed when he was thrown from his horse: "Between the stirrup and the ground, he mercy sought—and mercy found." One could, she pointed out to Marie with amused contempt, repent between yawns, so to speak—if it proved expedient. Tedious years weren't necessary. And even the slightest onset of tortured breathing would give her ample warning. Marie's anxious face went away.

It was restful to lie and watch the gnats dance in the

ray of sunlight. It wasn't necessary to look ahead too far. One should, for instance, look ahead only ten breaths. And when those were finished, one could start on the next ten. And so on, until it was night and one slept. It would be easy if it were done that way. Beneath the oxygen tent, she began to count drowsily: one two three four five six seven. And the seventh breath was as easy and determined as the others; but no more so.

Its only distinction lay in the fact that it was the last.

THE END